www.mascotbooks.com

The Weeping House

©2023 F. P. LaRue. All Rights Reserved. No part of this publication may be reproduced, stored in a retrieval system or transmitted in any form by any means electronic, mechanical, or photocopying, recording or otherwise without the permission of the author.

For more information, please contact:
Mascot Books, an imprint of Amplify Publishing Group
620 Herndon Parkway, Suite 220
Herndon, VA 20170
info@mascotbooks.com

Library of Congress Control Number: 2023912054
CPSIA Code: PRV0723A
ISBN-13: 978-1-63755-936-9

Printed in the United States

This book is dedicated to those who love adventure . . .
and who appreciate that life is all about the journey.

A SCARY SHIVERS MYSTERY

THE WEEPING HOUSE

F. P. LaRue

CHAPTER 1

I was in my secret room, mixing up a special powder. It would keep me and anyone I cared about safe from any evil creatures or people who would hurt us. I hoped it would anyway. I crushed a combination of herbs, spices, weeds, and thistle. I added a little of this and a little of that, along with some vinegar and baking soda that Mom had in the kitchen. You never know what will work.

Suddenly, gray smoke started to rise from my powder. I mixed everything in an old bowl Uncle John had given me a few years ago. There was a lot of smoke. The smoke encircled my head, and I coughed.

The basement door opened. "What are you doing

down there, Ollie?" asked Mom.

"Nothing," I said. "Just working on an experiment."

"Well, stop it," she said. "It's stinking up the house. It smells like a sewer."

"Okay," I said.

Mom was used to me doing different experiments. Overall, she and Dad supported my efforts, as long as I was careful.

I quickly doused the smoke with a dish towel. I wasn't sure exactly how I had made the smoke, but I was happy with this development. I shrugged. This special powder might come in handy in fighting off evildoers. You see, I call myself the Evil Destroyer.

My real name is Oliver. Ollie, to my family and friends. I am twelve years old and like to solve mysteries. Sometimes when I solve mysteries, I come across evil creatures or evil people. I always need to be ready, just in case there is trouble.

My parents tell me I have a sixth sense or a knack for figuring things out. I'm not sure what that means. I just know I like to solve different problems. I think I'm pretty good at it. I consider myself the best investigator who ever lived. I hope so, anyway.

The basement door opened again. "Mom, I took care

of it. Don't worry," I said. Then I heard footsteps coming down the stairs.

To my surprise, it was my two best friends in the world: Mellie and Scotty. I wasn't expecting to see them. I thought they both had family stuff going on today. I turned as they stopped at the door of my secret room.

"What's the password?" I asked.

"Evil Destroyer," said Mellie.

Scotty also followed with, "Evil Destroyer."

I stood aside so they could enter my room. I was glad they had come over. I liked them a lot. We are in the same grade. We have been friends since we were little kids. When I have a mystery to solve, I always ask them to help me.

Mellie is very practical. She only believes in what she can see and touch. She enjoys solving mysteries. She plays with her long hair when she is trying to figure things out or is concerned about something.

Scotty believes in things even if he can't see or touch them. When he gets nervous, he touches his glasses in some way. Sometimes he would clean or adjust them. He is kind of a chicken, but he still wants to solve mysteries.

We are a little bit different from each other, but the

same in our bond to always help each other. Whenever a situation arises when one or all of us are in trouble, we fist bump and say, "Friends Forever." This gives each of us confidence and helps us when solving mysteries.

Today, I wanted to ask them something and hoped they'd agree with my idea. "I'm glad you guys stopped by," I said. "Do you remember my Uncle John?"

"Yeah, I've met him before," said Scotty.

"Is he the one who researches the environment?" asked Mellie.

"Yes, he's the one," I said. "He's writing a book on plants and is going to take a trip and do some research in the mountains. He didn't mention exactly where, but he said it would take about half a day to get there. He rented a cabin and asked me if I wanted to go. I told him I thought that would be great."

"That does sound great," said Mellie. She glanced at Scotty.

"Yeah," Scotty said, looking at Mellie. Then they both looked at me.

I waited a moment, then smiled. "He said you both could come along, if you want." I barely got the words out before they started nudging and pushing me. We laughed and talked about the upcoming trip.

Before they left, Scotty asked, "This trip is just for fun, right? We're not looking into anything scary or anything like that, right?"

Mellie rolled her eyes in exasperation. "Nothing scary is going to happen. What could happen?"

Scotty looked at me expectantly. "Right?" he asked again.

"Right," I said.

I'm sure I won't need it, but I'll bring my special powder just in case, I thought. *While I am at it, I think I will bring my old mixing bowl and some ingredients . . . just in case.* But I didn't mention any of this to Scotty or Mellie.

Little did we know what was in store for us.

CHAPTER 2

A couple of days later, we were on our way to the cabin. Before we got to the cabin, Uncle John stopped at a bicycle rental store.

"I'm going to be busy most of the time we're here," he said. "I want you to have fun while I'm doing my research. I thought having a bike would make it easier for you to get around and go exploring."

"That's a great idea," I said.

"That would make things easier," said Mellie.

"I can't wait to go bike riding!" Scotty said.

Uncle John smiled and went to get us our bikes.

Uncle John is my mother's brother. He looks like my mom, but he's more on the skinny side (sorry, Mom). His hair is brown and shaggy. Thinning just a bit on the top.

We made it to the cabin without any problems. It was situated up in the mountains, like Uncle John had said. It was a little isolated, but no one minded because we were so excited about this trip. Not even Scotty.

The cabin was everything I hoped it would be. It was surrounded by oak and maple trees and many bushes. Various plants and weeds were mixed in with small twigs and leaves scattered on the ground. Some were filled with prickers or thorns, and others with various berries. It gave the area a natural but unkept or wild look.

The cabin was larger than I expected. It had four bedrooms, a living room, a dining room, and a study. The structure looked a bit worn down and rustic, but it fit in with the surroundings. Once we got settled in, Uncle John told us to meet him out back.

It was getting dark, and he was building a bonfire for us. We found some old chairs and settled around the fire pit. It didn't take Uncle John long to get the fire going.

"Why don't you get some sticks, and we can roast marshmallows?" he suggested.

We quickly searched the grounds and found what we needed. Soon we were all enjoying roasting marshmallows and sitting around the fire.

"Many years ago, the people in this area used fire to burn certain plants and bushes. It was thought that the smoke of these plants could ward off evil. The thornier and pricklier the better. It is a superstitious belief, but one they thought worked," Uncle John said.

"Is that one of the reasons why you decided to come here for your research?" I asked.

"The area is full of plants and trees that I want to investigate," Uncle John replied. "Also, many years ago, I came here on vacation. While I was here, I learned about the waterfall and caves in the area. I checked them out and collected some old relics and pottery. Nothing special, but it was fun.

"The cave system here is very elaborate and expands underground over several miles," Uncle John continued.

"Do you think we have a cave under this cabin?" Mellie asked.

"That would be fun to check out," I said.

"The cave system would be very old. It could collapse and bury us alive," said Scotty.

"Not to worry, Scotty," Uncle John said. "I'm not sure the cave system expands to here. But even if it did, the entrance would have been sealed off when the house was built."

"Why?" I asked.

"For safety reasons," he explained. "Anyway, the waterfall and above-ground caves will be interesting. I thought you might enjoy it."

"I'm already enjoying it," I said. "Being out here at night, is the perfect time for a ghost story. How about it? Does anyone know a good ghost story?"

"Not really," said Mellie.

Scotty quickly shook his head. "I try not to listen to ghost stories."

"I don't have a ghost story exactly," said Uncle John. "But as I was researching the area, I heard a story that was kind of a mystery, and it happened right here." He stared straight ahead, then continued. "No one really knows exactly what happened, but as the story goes, a young woman named Eleanor fell in love with a young but poor man named Robert. They would meet at her house in the woods, supposedly somewhere around here. Another suitor, named Victor, was also interested in Eleanor. Victor was from a rich and powerful family. He cherished his money and material possessions. Above all, he loved power. Eleanor told Victor she loved someone else. But he wouldn't take 'no' for an answer. Victor didn't take her rejection well. If he couldn't have

Eleanor, no one could. So, Victor put a curse on her. She was to stay in that house forever—always looking for her lover but never finding him."

Scotty noisily gulped down his marshmallow. We all looked at him, making sure he was okay.

Then Uncle John continued. "Victor did something to Robert, too. I don't know what. But whatever Victor did to him, Robert couldn't help Eleanor because of it. Both of them were trapped in their own way. They longed to be together but were eternally forced apart. It is thought that Victor still roams the area, even to this day, spitefully happy with what he did. Over the years, people have said they have heard crying or sobbing coming from that house. They call it the Weeping House." Uncle John looked at us, smiled, then shrugged.

No one said anything for a few minutes. I was thinking it was a sad story. Mellie and Scotty looked lost in their thoughts. Then I asked, "It's just a story, right?"

"I think it's kind of a local legend," said Uncle John. "But some people believe it to be true." We must have looked worried because then he said, "You know, as time goes on, stories get exaggerated. I've never seen that house, and I don't know anyone who has. I wouldn't put too much thought into it."

"Yeah, you're right," I said. "It's just an old story anyway."

"Yeah, that sounds right," said Mellie.

Scotty said nothing. He just kept looking around at the shadows caused by the fire. He looked as if he was expecting Victor to appear.

CHAPTER 3

The next day, Uncle John said he would be doing research and would be busy throughout the day. We wanted to go adventuring and asked him about the area.

"It's pretty secluded," he said. "There aren't many houses around that I know of. The waterfall and caves I mentioned are not far from here. That might be something you could check out. I know there are well-marked trails around here. You should be okay."

"Maybe we should bring some water and snacks," suggested Mellie.

"That's a good idea," said Scotty. "I'll go and get them."

Before leaving, Uncle John turned to us. "Needless

to say, be careful," he said.

Excited to get started, I said, "We will. Don't worry." Little did we know a lot of worries were coming our way.

But at the moment, we couldn't wait to explore and have fun. We found a bike trail and rode our bikes for a while, enjoying being outside. Even Scotty seemed relaxed and without a care in the world.

We were talking and laughing and soon came to what could have been another trail. But this trail was not marked. There was no trail sign, and it was not clear of debris like the one we were on. It looked overgrown, and twigs, weeds, and leaves were scattered all over it.

"Well, we can stay on the trail we're on," I said. "Or we could try this one." I pointed to the unmarked one.

Mellie and Scotty looked questioningly at each other. Mellie shrugged. "Let's try the one you're pointing at, Ollie. It might be more fun."

Scotty looked at both trails. "I'm not sure." But he was still caught up in our carefree time, so he said, "Okay, why not?"

We all started to laugh and took off down the unmarked trail. It was overgrown and a bit difficult to ride on. Then, a little way down the trail, a couple of large branches blocked the way. I got off my bike and approached the branches.

"I think we should just go back and ride the trail we were on," said Scotty. "The one that was marked."

"Just a minute," I said. "Something isn't right about this."

"You're right," said Mellie. "These branches didn't naturally break off a tree. It looks like they were deliberately cut off."

"Definitely. The cuts are all the same. They are all straight, clean cuts," I said. "These branches were purposely put here to block the way. To make sure that anyone wouldn't go down this path."

"That means someone or something doesn't want us here," Scotty said nervously. "All the more reason to go back to the marked trail."

"I think we should continue on this path and see why someone wanted to block it," I said.

"I'm willing to go on a bit farther," said Mellie.

"Okay, but if we see anything scary or creepy, I think we should go back," said Scotty.

"Alright. Let's go," I said.

We walked our bikes around the branches, got back on them, and continued riding on the old trail. I led the way, with Mellie behind me, and Scotty reluctantly following her. A while later, the woods opened up into a clearing. An old house stood there.

"I thought Uncle John said there weren't many houses in the area," said Mellie.

"Well, it's not on the beaten path. Maybe no one knows it's here," I suggested.

As we got closer, I said, "It doesn't appear that anyone lives here. Let's check it out. After all, we are here to have fun and explore. Can't hurt to look around a little bit."

"It might," said Scotty. "Maybe we should just keep going." He peered around nervously, surveying the area. "Something doesn't seem right here."

I was starting to feel something wasn't quite right either. I gazed around. As I walked up to the steps, I turned my head and stared at the dead trees and branches near the side of the house. I felt like I was being pulled to notice something there. I stared for a minute but didn't see anything unusual. Just trees and branches. I shook my head.

"What's wrong?" asked Mellie.

"I don't know," I said. "I just had a funny feeling when I looked at the trees and branches over there . . . like someone or something was trying to get my attention. It was probably nothing." I shrugged. Everything

seemed okay.

"It's just an old house," I said. "C'mon." We looked at each other and slowly approached the building.

The house was badly in need of repair. The paint was peeling off. The shutters were hanging down. The windows were almost black from dirt and grime. All the bushes and plants were overgrown. Dead trees surrounded the house. Their dead, rotting limbs were lying on the ground. It appeared that some smaller trees had tried to grow but, for whatever reason, had just given up and died.

On the side of the house, a bunch of what looked like tree limbs were sticking up out of the ground. They looked like old, withered arms topped with clawed, broken hands reaching up toward the sky, as if they didn't want to give up. But they weren't sticking straight up. They were actually leaning toward the house. I found that odd.

Scotty brushed up against one. I saw that his sleeve was wet. He didn't notice it at first. When he did realize it was wet, he rubbed at it absently.

"This house has been here a long time," I said.

"I bet at one time it was beautiful," observed Mellie.

"By the looks of it now, whatever its story is, it can't

be good," said Scotty.

I went to take a closer look at the house.

"What are you doing?" asked Scotty.

"Just getting a closer look," I said.

"Yeah, I'd like to check this out, too," commented Mellie.

"I don't think that's a good idea," said Scotty.

"You always say that," said Mellie.

Scotty stuck his tongue out at her, frowned, then ran to catch up with Mellie and me.

As we started up the steps toward the front door, each one creaked and cracked as if complaining about our intrusion. *Or are they trying to stop or warn us?* I wondered.

We glanced at each other.

"Noisy, aren't they?" asked Mellie.

Scotty didn't say anything.

I just smiled at Mellie.

As we got to the top of the porch, I thought I heard something. "Be quiet," I said. "Can you hear that?"

With everyone quiet, we heard the faint sound of someone crying. It sounded like a woman sobbing almost uncontrollably.

"That's the saddest thing I've ever heard," said Mellie.

"Um . . . I think we should go now," said Scotty.

Mellie went to peek in the windows. "I can't really see anything," she said. "It's very dark inside." She returned to where Scotty and I were standing.

I knocked on the door, hard. But, as I expected, there was no answer. Then I reached for the doorknob. "Ouch," I yelped in surprise and pain.

"What happened?" asked Mellie.

"Did something bite you?" asked Scotty, alarmed, his voice rising.

"I don't think anything bit me," I said, rubbing my hand. "It felt more like an electrical shock."

"Let's get out of here!" Scotty said.

"That's a good idea," I agreed.

Mellie nodded in approval.

As we turned to go down the stairs, the door started to shake violently. Mellie, Scotty, and I froze, not understanding what was happening. Paint and wood chips from the door fell quickly to the ground in mounds.

"Please help me!" cried a woman's voice.

Mellie, Scotty, and I flew down the steps. We got on our bikes, and raced down the old trail as fast as we could.

CHAPTER 4

We made it into town. We talked about what happened the whole way.

"How's your hand?" asked Mellie.

"It still tingles, but it's okay, I guess," I said, flexing my fingers.

"None of that should have happened," Scotty said, shaking his head. "You don't get electric shocks through doors, and doors don't just start shaking on their own."

"And what about the woman's voice? And the sobbing?" asked Mellie. "She sounded like she really needed help."

"I know. It sure was creepy," I said. "I really wasn't expecting that."

"You can say that again," said Scotty.

"Something is going on over there," I said. "I would like to know what it is."

"You would," said Scotty.

"Here's the general store," I said as we pulled up in front of it. It was a medium-sized building made of wood. It looked like it had been around a long time. "I want to buy an area map showing the waterfall and caves. We can go there when we're done here."

"That's a great idea," said Mellie.

"This is going to be fun," said Scotty.

As we entered the store, I thought about what had happened at the house. Mellie must have been thinking about it as well because she said, "I think what just happened at that house has to do with that curse Uncle John told us about."

"I thought that the story of the young woman, her lover, and the rejected suitor was just that—a story," I said. "But now I'm not so sure. I think someone might need our help . . . again."

Mellie nodded.

Scotty glanced from me to Mellie. He was frowning. "Hey, guys," he said, "we're here to have fun, remember?"

"I know," I started to say, "but . . ."

A man who had been stocking the shelves overheard us talking. He said he was the store owner. "Are you kids talking about the sad story of the young woman and her lover who disappeared at the Weeping House?" he asked.

"Yes, we were," I said. "Do you know if it's true?"

"I don't know if it's true or not," said the store owner. "But many people here believe it is. Strange things have happened at that house. People stay away from there."

"Can you tell us about it?" asked Mellie.

"I could tell you what I know, but the person you really should talk to is Old Henry. He's been living here for years and knows all there is to know about all the stories and happenings that have gone on around here. The good and the bad." He looked around for a moment, then added, "Mostly the bad."

"How do we find him?" I asked.

"He usually sits outside on the front porch of the store, minding his own business. I don't know if he'll talk to you. He doesn't really like to talk to strangers." The store owner scratched his head. "He doesn't really like talking to anyone, especially kids. But you can ask him, I guess."

I found the map and paid for it. I thanked the store

owner. Once that was done, I turned to Scotty and Mellie. "Well, what do you think? Should we go and talk to Old Henry?" I asked.

"Can't hurt," said Mellie.

"Oh, great. Famous last words," said Scotty.

We left the store and saw Old Henry on the front porch, just like the store owner said. He was sleeping and snoring. An old torn hat covered his eyes.

We approached him. "Mister? Excuse me, Mister? Can we ask you a few questions about this town?" I asked as politely as I could.

But he didn't move. His snores grew louder.

"I don't think he wants to be bothered," observed Mellie.

"I think you're right," I said. "But we need to find out about the crying woman and that strange house. And whether it might be the Weeping House. We can go back there to check it out again."

When Old Henry heard us mention the Weeping House, he pushed his hat back. "What do you know about it?" he asked in a raspy voice.

I told him about going up to the house and what had happened. I explained what we knew about Eleanor, Robert, and Victor.

"Yes, that all is true. Strange things do happen at that house. But not only there. There is more to the story. A lot more. The caves are also a part of it."

"Can you please tell us what you know?" I asked.

Old Henry peered intently at us. At first, it didn't seem like he was going to tell us anything. Then he began. "It was rumored that Victor's family practiced black magic and that Victor learned all he could from them. No one really believed that. Eleanor believed it, though. She knew Victor was capable of anything.

"When Eleanor tried to avoid Victor, she hid in the caves. She was afraid of Victor and felt threatened by him. It was said that Eleanor kept a diary detailing her fears. Some have speculated that she also included clues about what to do if she ever went missing. Supposedly, she hid the diary in the caves in case something happened to her. But it was never found.

"No one took seriously that she wanted to marry Robert. He was poor and couldn't offer her much. She didn't care. They loved each other deeply. Her family and friends told her how lucky she was that Victor was interested in her. He was wealthy and had a lot to offer. But Eleanor knew that Victor was evil. She told people. But they didn't believe her. Or they didn't want to believe that such things were possible. I don't know which.

"As you mentioned, Victor put a curse on Robert. What you need to know is that Robert was near and knew Eleanor was in the house. He could hear her crying and sighing. But he couldn't do anything about it."

"If Robert was near and could hear her crying and sighing, how come he couldn't help her?" I asked.

"I don't know," said Old Henry. "But he couldn't."

"If Robert was outside, he would have helped her," Scotty remarked.

"I agree. If Robert could have helped her, he would have," said Old Henry. "But Victor ensured that he couldn't."

"Didn't anyone see him outside?" Mellie asked.

"Nope. Robert was never seen again," said Old Henry. "Eventually, all three of them disappeared."

Old Henry stopped. He looked like he was debating on what to tell us next. After a few moments, he said, "You got off easy. Sometimes people who have gone there disappear. Investigations were made, but no one knows what happened to them."

"That sounds strange," said Mellie.

"People don't just disappear," said Scotty.

I didn't know what to believe.

"Do you believe all of this?" I asked.

Old Henry stared right into my eyes. "It doesn't matter if I believe it or not. *It's true!* Just because you don't believe it doesn't mean it's not true. Stay away from that house." He frowned at us. He then pointed his gnarled finger at us and said, "You have been warned!"

CHAPTER 5

After leaving Old Henry, we walked down the street. We wanted to talk over what Old Henry had told us.

"Wow! He was a bit intense," said Mellie.

"It goes along with what Uncle John told us," I said.

"It does, but it's all over now," said Scotty.

"Is it?" I asked. "You saw and heard what happened at that house."

Mellie and Scotty didn't answer. Mellie was gazing straight ahead, twirling a piece of hair around her finger. Scotty was cleaning his glasses. I knew the whole situation was unsettling. It was for me, too.

"Look, we're here to have fun, right?" I said, hoping to lighten the moment. "We don't need to think about this right now. Let's look at the map and find out where the caves and the waterfall are."

Mellie quit twirling her hair and smiled. Scotty stopped cleaning his glasses. He grinned and said, "Now you're talking."

We shook off our uneasiness about what had happened earlier.

We studied the map and found the route we would take to the caves and the waterfall. We returned to our bikes and followed the map. It took some time, but we found them.

"There's the waterfall," cried Mellie. "It's beautiful!"

We just stopped and scanned the area. It was very scenic. Large trees and various-sized bushes grew around the caves and waterfall. Rocks of different lengths and sizes surrounded the area and made a natural barrier in front of the caves. For a while, we just stared. We started to relax and enjoy ourselves. We nibbled on some snacks and drank some water we brought with us.

"Come on," I said. "Time to explore and have fun." We got off our bikes and made our way to the side of the waterfall.

"I see an opening," said Mellie, and she started for it.

Scotty and I followed behind her. The opening was

very narrow, so we had to squeeze through it single file to get behind the waterfall. But we did with no trouble.

As we entered the cave, it was dark. We needed to wait for our eyes to adjust. After a few minutes, I said, "I can see a little bit better now."

"I can see better, too," said Mellie.

"Me too," said Scotty. "It's big. Bigger than what I thought it would be."

The cave was cool, and there was some dampness in the air. There was a smell of wet rocks. It was otherworldly, but we were happy to be there. We laughed and joked, excited to have fun and explore. There were tunnels that went to the right, straight ahead, and to the left.

"Which tunnel, guys?" Mellie asked.

Scotty and I looked at each other. He looked like he was trying to decide which way to go. Then I pointed to the middle tunnel. It appeared wide and easy to follow. I glanced at Scotty. He nodded.

"This one it is," said Mellie. We started down the tunnel. We had our flashlights with us and turned them on.

After a while, we came to a sign on a stand that read, "STOP! DANGER! DO NOT GO BEYOND THIS POINT!"

"Oh well," I said. "Time to turn around."

As we started to go back, we heard a strange sound.

"What was that?" asked Scotty.

"I don't know," I said. I was more curious than concerned. We listened closely.

"It sounded like a moan," Scotty said nervously.

"It kind of sounded like a book hitting the ground," said Mellie.

Scotty and I gaped at her in disbelief. Mellie shrugged. I took a step toward where the sound had come from.

"Where are you going?" asked Scotty. I'm sure he knew the answer but didn't want to hear it.

"I'm going to go check it out," I replied, matter-of-factly.

"Maybe we shouldn't do that," suggested Scotty.

"It's probably nothing," said Mellie.

"With our luck, it's probably something," said Scotty.

"Maybe someone fell and needs our help. We should at least go a little farther," I said. Scotty thought about it and finally nodded.

"Hello, is anyone there?" Mellie called out.

We followed the tunnel toward the sound.

A little way up the path, Scotty peeked behind him. "The hair on the back of my neck is sticking up," he said. He rubbed his neck. "It feels like someone or something is watching us." He looked at Mellie and me as if waiting for us to say something.

"I don't feel anything," said Mellie.

"I don't either," I said.

"Still . . ." Scotty started, when we heard a different sound. We stopped. It came from above us.

"That sounds like scraping," Mellie said.

Before Scotty or I could answer, something came flying out of a hole in the wall. I wasn't sure what it was, but it sure startled us. We all cried out in fear and surprise.

CHAPTER 6

"**O**nly a bat," I noted. My voice shook a little.

"'*Only a bat*'?" exclaimed Scotty. I knew he was creeped out. Who wouldn't be?

"Bats are to be expected in caves," said Mellie, although she appeared a little pale.

We stood there peering around, afraid to move. We glanced up at the ceiling and the walls. After a couple of minutes, nothing else happened. All seemed quiet.

"Maybe we've had enough excitement for today," I said. "What do you think of heading back?"

Before Mellie and Scotty could answer, we heard another sound. A different sound from before. Laughter. Faintly at first, then louder. Evil laughter. It was all around us. It became so loud I could feel the air pulsating on my skin.

Mellie, Scotty, and I took off running along the path. After a while, I slowed down and stopped. "It doesn't sound as loud as before," I said.

"Hey," Mellie exclaimed, as she fell down. Her knees were scraped up a little. She looked around, but, neither Scotty nor I were close to her. Scotty and I went to help her up.

Mellie was brushing dirt off her clothes. I examined her scrapes. "Are you okay?" I asked.

"I'm okay," Mellie reassured us.

The evil laughter stopped. We looked at each other, not sure what to think.

"What was that?" asked Mellie.

"*Who* was that?" asked Scotty.

"Someone was trying to get our attention," I said.

"Well, they got it!" Scotty hollered. "Let's get out of here!"

Mellie agreed. "I think you're right, Scotty. Besides the creepy laughter, something strange is going on here."

"What do you mean?" I asked.

Mellie shook her head. "I'm not sure how I fell. For a second, I thought someone pushed me."

Scotty and I looked at each other, trying to figure out what had happened.

"We were ahead of you," Scotty said. "So, it wasn't us."

"I guess I must have tripped on something," said Mellie. "But I don't know . . . I could have sworn . . ."

We searched around but couldn't find anything Mellie could have tripped on.

"But I did see something when I fell. Something caught my eye," Mellie said.

"What was it?" I asked.

"I'm not sure," she said, "but something."

Mellie searched to the right of the path we had been running on. She walked closer to the wall there. The wall was brown with bits of rocks and sand embedded in it. Mellie examined it closer.

"I thought I saw something shiny or glittery out of the corner of my eye . . . yes!" she shouted, brushing away some of the rocks and sand. Part of a thin gold chain was visible. "What is this?" she asked.

"Probably just a piece of metal or a souvenir someone dropped years ago," suggested Scotty.

Mellie gently cleared away the area around the chain. She tugged on the chain, but it wouldn't budge. The more she brushed at the wall, the more rocks and sand tumbled down, but the chain stayed lodged in the wall.

"I can't pull it out," said Mellie, a little frustrated, as she struggled with it.

"Be careful," I said. "You don't want to break it."

"You would easily miss this unless you were looking for it," said Mellie. "I wouldn't have seen it if I hadn't fallen."

"Here, try this." Scotty opened the pocketknife he always carried with him and handed it to her.

"Thanks," said Mellie. She worked the blade around the chain. Scotty and I tried to help. We dug around the area where the chain was with our hands and Scotty's pocketknife. I was curious to see what we'd found. Suddenly, more rocks and sand came tumbling down at our feet.

"Look out!" I yelled. I was worried that the wall was falling apart and would cover us. We ran a few feet backward. Dust and dirt swirled around us. When they finally cleared, the gold chain was lying in the rubble at our feet.

"I wonder how that got stuck in the wall," Scotty pondered.

Mellie picked up the chain. But she quickly dropped it.

"What's wrong?" I asked.

"I don't know," said Mellie. "It felt kind of funny in my hand. Like a tingling feeling." She seemed a little concerned. She was opening and closing her hand and rubbing it.

I picked up the chain and held it for a few seconds. "I don't feel anything." I gave the chain to Scotty.

Scotty took the chain with his thumb and one finger. It seemed he wasn't taking any chances. After a few moments, he grasped it fully in his hand. "I don't feel anything weird," he said, as he tightened his grip on it. "Here, try it again." He gave the chain to Mellie.

Mellie hesitated, then took the chain. As soon as she touched it, she said, "When I touch this, I definitely feel a tingling sensation. That's just weird." Her eyes grew wide. "Don't you think that's weird?" she asked.

"That is definitely weird," said Scotty.

I scratched my head. "I agree. It must mean something, though."

"What?" asked Mellie as she nervously twirled a strand of hair around her finger.

"I'm not sure we want to find out," said Scotty.

"How would it even get stuck in the wall?" asked Mellie.

"I'm not sure." I peered closely at the wall. I started

digging at it again. "I don't think—" I began to say, and then the wall started to rumble. Rocks and dirt fell from it.

We stepped back. Suddenly, there was a huge crash and the wall completely collapsed, leaving a gaping hole where it had been!

CHAPTER 7

We quickly stepped back from the rubble that had been the wall. Once I knew everyone was safe, I shared, "I was just about to say that the wall didn't seem solid. I guess I was right."

"Look, it's another tunnel that leads farther into the caves," said Mellie.

She had dropped the chain when the wall collapsed. We had forgotten about it for the moment. I noticed it on the ground and picked it up. We hadn't had a chance to really look at it. It was gold and looked to be a necklace. It was a simple design, with small gold circles attached to one another.

"Look, there's a locket at the end of the chain," said Mellie.

The locket was gold like the chain but round and flat. In its center was a large blue jewel in the shape of a triangle. I gave the chain back to Mellie. The blue jewel began to glimmer. "It's tingling again," she said, but she held onto it this time.

"Wow!" I exclaimed. "Mellie, this is not just a locket. I think you've found an amulet."

Mellie looked uncomfortable and lowered her hand, like she was going to drop the chain.

"No, don't drop it, Mellie. I think it's okay," I said. "I can take it if you want me to."

Mellie handed me the chain. "I don't like that it tingles only in my hand and not in either of yours," she said.

"Does it hurt you?" I asked.

"No, it doesn't hurt exactly," she said. "It's more of a persistent vibrating feeling."

I examined the amulet more closely. "For whatever reason, I think it's trying to get your attention. I don't think it's trying to hurt you. It could have done so already. I'll hold on to it for now if you want me to."

"I would appreciate it," Mellie said, smiling and looking relieved.

"What's an amulet?" Scotty asked. "It looks old."

"It does look old," I said.

Scotty and Mellie looked at me expectantly.

"An amulet," I began, "is something that has special powers. It is often a piece of jewelry. This amulet obviously has some connection with you, Mellie." Before I could continue, we heard an odd noise.

"What is that?" asked Scotty.

Looking around, I said, "I'm not sure."

We heard it again. It sounded like some type of creepy clicking and snapping. Hundreds of them, all happening at once.

"It sounds like it is coming from behind us," said Mellie.

The clicking and snapping grew louder.

"I don't care where it's coming from," cried Scotty. "Let's get out of here!"

CHAPTER 8

We stopped in our tracks and turned to go back the way we had come. Hundreds of translucent white creatures were crawling toward us on the path we needed to take. I felt like I was watching a horror movie. But I knew I wasn't. We could see their bones through their skin. Their mouths opened and closed, their tiny sharp teeth clicking and snapping. Their bodies were round and flat. They were about eight inches long and walked on eight legs. The bottom of each leg was pointed and dug into the ground as they walked.

We stared in horror as the creatures crawled toward us with increasing speed. Transparent liquid dripped from between their teeth. They didn't seem to have any eyes! Even without eyes, they clearly had one purpose: to get Mellie, Scotty, and me! To *eat* us!

"It's time to go," I yelled.

"Which way?" screeched Scotty.

I looked around. There was only one way we could go. I quickly dropped the chain into my pocket. Just before we turned to run down the new tunnel we had found, one of the no-eyed, boney creatures jumped and landed on Scotty's shoe. It opened its mouth and clamped on Scotty's shoe with its tiny, sharp teeth.

"It's biting my shoe!" yelled Scotty in disgust. He tried to kick it off. It didn't budge. The creature just clung onto Scotty's shoe with its sharp teeth, biting and shaking from side to side. Again, Scotty tried harder to kick it off. That time it worked. Scotty stomped on it. Killing it. The creature made a high-pitched shriek.

We ran down the path as fast as we could, fear pushing us forward. We weren't watching where we were going. We just knew we had to get out of there. Fast. We could hear the creatures behind us. The cave was getting even darker. Even with our three flashlights, we could barely see where we were going. We came to a fork in the tunnels.

"Which way?" yelled Mellie.

I pointed to the tunnel on the left. We could hear the creatures getting closer, the never-ending clicking and snapping of their teeth. We ran faster. Then the tunnel just stopped. We were staring at a rock wall on three sides of us. "Oh no!" I yelled. "It's a dead end!" We stopped. Mellie and Scotty were staring at me in horror.

"Oh no," moaned Scotty. The creepy clicking and snapping was getting louder and closer. It sounded like there were even more of them than before!

"Let's go back to the other tunnel. It's our only chance!" I yelled.

As we took a few steps forward, we stopped in shock. Our exit was blocked by the no-eyed, boney creatures!

"Now what?" hollered Scotty.

I looked around frantically, trying to come up with an escape route.

The no-eyed, boney creatures crawled and edged steadily closer. Slowly. Inching their way toward us. In the dim light, it looked like they were smiling. The clicking and snapping grew faster and louder as the creatures realized their quarry was trapped. They had us right where they wanted us. Mellie, Scotty, and I stepped back.

"Ollie, what are we going to do?" yelled Mellie.

Our backs were pressed against the wall. I could feel the cold walls through my clothes. Our bodies were huddled together in fear.

"I don't know . . ." I began to say.

Suddenly, the feeling of the cold hard wall pressed against my shoulders seemed to disappear. It was as if my shoulders were free. The next thing I knew, I fell backward into the wall. Just like that, I was gone.

Scotty and Mellie screamed my name. For one agonized moment, time seemed to stop.

I was able to extend my arms through the wall. I grabbed Mellie and Scotty and pulled them inside the wall, just as the creatures viciously attacked.

CHAPTER 9

Mellie, Scotty, and I fell to the floor, shouting in terror. We could faintly hear the creatures shrieking angrily, frustrated that their prey had gotten away. They were crushing each other, splattering themselves into the rock wall, but could not penetrate it.

We stood up, looking around quickly. There were four walls and a ceiling in need of repair. There was some furniture. It looked like we were in a room, in a home. But who's home? Where?

"That was a close one," Scotty sighed.

"I can't believe we got away," Mellie said. "Ollie, where are we?"

"I'm not sure," I said. But I had a weird feeling. I

thought to myself, *Could we be in Eleanor's house?*

"How'd we get here?" asked Scotty, shaking his head as if to clear it. "We were just in the caves, with those . . . those . . . *things.*"

"I'm not sure," I said, perplexed. "There must be some type of connecting door or passage here. It must have let us through when we were leaning back somehow."

"The last thing I remember you were pulling us through the wall," Mellie said.

"Yeah, me too," said Scotty, cleaning his glasses.

As we were talking, I inspected the wall we had come through. I couldn't see any lines or markings on the wall to indicate a door or passageway was there.

"I don't know," I said, shaking my head. "I don't know how we came through the wall. I don't see a door or opening anywhere."

I went over what happened in my mind. Finally, I said, "My back was pressed against the cold, hard rock wall. Then I couldn't feel the rock wall. Next, I thought I felt one of you grab my shirt and pull me into the wall. But you were on either side of me. I felt someone or something pulling the neck of my shirt, and I fell through the wall and grabbed both of you. And here we are."

"Yes, here we are," said Scotty, "and now we should

go." He took a step to find the front door.

"Wait a minute," I said.

I looked around and saw we were in a living room. There were a couple of chairs and a table. There was a fireplace with a large portrait of a young woman hanging above the mantle. The windows in the room were nearly black, and you could barely see outside.

"This might be Eleanor's house," I said. "Remember, the windows were black. And the portrait over the fireplace could be Eleanor."

"I think you are right," said Mellie.

"And I think that's all the more reason to leave," Scotty said.

"Since we're here, I think we should check things out," I said.

"Yes," agreed Mellie. "It can't hurt."

"I knew that was coming," Scotty grumbled. "Ouch!" he said as Mellie pinched his arm.

"We need to find out all the information we can to help Eleanor and Robert," I said.

"I guess," Scotty agreed reluctantly, following Mellie and me to the center of the room. "I have to at least sit down." He went to the nearest chair and plopped down into it, giving a long sigh of relief. The chair was oversized

with thick cushions. It was near the fireplace.

Mellie and I scanned around the room. We weren't exactly sure what we were searching for. I thought maybe we might find something that might help us with this mystery.

I scrutinized the portrait carefully. The woman in the picture was pretty with dark hair. Her eyes were large and a soft brown, with long black lashes. She had a sweet smile and held a handkerchief in her hand.

I know that is Eleanor, I thought.

I pulled out the amulet from my pocket to see if there was a picture inside it. I tried to open it but couldn't.

"Let me see it," Mellie said. I gave it to her. Like before, it tingled in her hand, but she didn't seem to be afraid of it now. She examined it and then turned it over, looking for a hidden clasp or button. She didn't find anything. "I'm going to try one more time," she said. She pressed down on the top of it . . . and it opened up. "I can't believe it," she said.

Inside was a sepia picture of a young woman and a young man. "I think it's her," Mellie said.

We looked from the amulet to the portrait. "It is the same person," I said. "And that's probably Robert." I pointed to the other picture in the amulet.

"He's handsome," said Mellie.

Robert had wavy, dark hair and beautiful eyes.

Suddenly, the amulet started to vibrate in Mellie's hand. Her hand began to shake, and she almost dropped it. As her fist tightened on the amulet, her fingers brushed the large blue jewel. A white mist rose from it and drifted toward the portrait. Mellie, Scotty, and I were too surprised to move.

The mist swirled around the portrait of Eleanor. The ghostly face of Eleanor came alive in the picture! Her features softened and became animated. We couldn't believe what we were seeing!

It was as if we were watching a movie screen.

Eleanor spoke from the picture. "Somehow, Victor found out Robert and I were going to run off. The night we were to leave, Victor stormed into my house. I remembered about the amulet. But it was too late. I had hidden it in the cave.

"Understanding the situation at once, Robert rushed to Victor, hoping to reason with him. Victor pointed his finger at Robert and raged, 'You want to be with Eleanor, so be it.' Victor then pointed at me and shouted, 'You want to be with him, then you'll have your wish.' He chanted some words I didn't understand. Then Robert just disappeared.

"'*Robert!*' I screamed. Victor sneered, 'You will always be close to Robert but always apart. He is near and knows you are close. But he can't ever help you. And you can't help him. You are cursed to stay locked in this house forever. Anyone who tries to help you will be destroyed!' And with that, Victor disappeared. In agony, I screamed again, '*Robert!*'"

Eleanor collapsed, sobbing uncontrollably. Finally, above her crying, we heard Victor's evil, satisfied laughter. Then total silence. The picture froze there, with Eleanor weeping.

We were stunned at what had just happened. Then before we could gather our thoughts, Eleanor's face became animated again. She was looking directly at us.

"Thank you for wanting to help me, but you are in grave danger," she said. "You are now a part of this. In the past, Victor destroyed anyone who dared to help me. He must feel that you are a threat to him. I can sense his rage when you are near. You must find my diary. In it are clues on how to destroy him. If he is not destroyed," she smiled sadly, "you will be." Eleanor looked behind her. Only she could see what was coming.

Eleanor's face quickly faded. The original portrait

returned to the frame. Then we heard a sickening laugh. It was the same evil laughter we had heard in the cave. Instantly, a man's face replaced Eleanor's in the portrait. He had dark hair and eyes. An aristocratic nose. He was very handsome, but the evil that emanated from him was so intense I could feel it go through me. It felt cold, dark, and lifeless. It was dreadful. We all shivered.

A realization dawned on me. "I guess that must be Victor," I whispered.

Mellie and Scotty could only nod.

"You have no business here," he snarled. "Eleanor is mine." Then his arm sprang out of the picture. He reached out toward Scotty. Victor grabbed Scotty by the front of his shirt, squeezing tightly! We were all in such shock, we couldn't move. We couldn't believe what we were seeing.

"Help!" Scotty yelped, as he twisted and struggled, trying to free himself.

Victor held on tight and was slowly pulling him toward the picture. It looked like Victor was going to pull Scotty *into* the picture!

I grabbed Scotty by the waist and yanked as hard as I could. But Victor was able to keep dragging Scotty toward the picture. Mellie grabbed me by the waist. We pulled hard, but Victor was strong. Scotty's head was almost in the picture. Mellie and I yanked harder, but the top of Scotty's head disappeared into the picture.

"Ugh," It sounded like Scotty was being pulled underwater. It was awful to hear.

"Ollie!" Mellie yelled out in panic.

"Friends Forever!" I bellowed.

A renewed sense of strength overcame me. I took a deep breath and pulled with all my willpower. From the resolve I could see on Mellie's face, she was doing the same thing. That gave us enough extra strength that, together, we were able to pull Scotty out of Victor's grasp. We all fell to the floor, exhausted.

A cold black mist came up from the floor, surrounding us. It smelled like the ashes of the dead. It chilled me to the bone.

"He's not done with us yet," I hollered. "Let's go!"

We ran out the front door and didn't look back.

CHAPTER 10

That night, back at our cabin, I didn't sleep well. I don't think any of us did. Nightmares flowed in and out, disrupting my dreams. In the morning, we woke to bright sunshine. We sat at the kitchen table. Quietly eating our breakfast. I had an uncomfortable, uncertain feeling. I was thinking about what happened the day before and what our next steps might be.

Uncle John came into the kitchen and got a bowl of cereal. He sat down at the table with us. "How's the exploring going?" he asked with a smile.

"Pretty good," I said. "There's a lot here to explore. We've been busy, that's for sure." I smiled at Mellie and Scotty.

"Have fun, but don't overdo it," he said, as he finished his cereal. "I'll be back later." As he was leaving, he turned to us. "Be careful out there. Don't let the ghosts get you," he joked.

"Too late for that," Scotty muttered. But Uncle John had already left.

"We should go over what happened," I said. "We found an amulet that appears to belong to Eleanor."

"What about those creatures?" asked Mellie, shivering.

"Yeah," said Scotty. "I've never seen anything like them. No eyes!"

"Some creatures in caves adapt to not having light," I explained. "They don't have eyes because they don't have to see the way we do. They can feel vibrations or sense movement. Or they use smell to survive or find their prey."

"Why were they coming after us?" asked Mellie. "We didn't do anything to them."

"I'm not sure," I said. "Maybe they wanted us out of their area. Or maybe they felt threatened."

"I sure felt threatened," Scotty interjected.

"Me too," Mellie said. "I also felt they were deliberately coming after us. To hurt us."

"To eat us," Scotty agreed, looking like he was going to be sick.

"I agree with you," I said. "It sure looked like they wanted to hurt us."

"What about the one that landed on my shoe? It didn't want to let go. It was trying to bite me!" Scotty's voice was becoming more high-pitched. "I couldn't get it off my shoe either. I think there is still some stuck under my shoe."

"I heard them splatter on the wall after we escaped," Mellie said. "Yuck. They didn't care if they died or not. They wanted to get us no matter what."

"They were very aggressive," I said. "I wonder if Victor had anything to do with them." Mellie and Scotty looked like they were thinking the same thing.

Remembering how Victor grabbed him from the picture, Scotty said, "Victor must be very powerful to almost pull me into the picture." He gulped loudly.

Mellie nodded. "Eleanor's amulet must also be powerful to bring her to the picture."

"Eleanor told us to find her diary," I said. "It looks like that's what we have to do. We are a part of this now."

"Whether we want to be or not," moaned Scotty. "That's just *great*."

"But we don't have any idea where to start looking," Mellie said.

"I know," I said. "We'll just have to figure it out."

"I wanted to help Eleanor and Robert," Mellie groaned. "But I didn't think anything bad would happen to us."

"I think we're in over our heads this time," said Scotty.

"That's when we do our best work." I smiled, trying to be encouraging.

Mellie and Scotty looked at each other. "I'll take your word for it," Mellie said, shaking her head as she adjusted her hair.

"Sure, it is," Scotty said, as he wiped the sweat from his glasses.

We all knew we were heading back to the caves.

CHAPTER 11

We gathered some supplies for our trip back to the caves. Flashlights, water, and some snacks. We put them in a backpack and gave it to Scotty.

As we approached our bikes, I said, "Wait a minute." I hurried back inside, got my special powder, and returned to the bikes.

"This is a special powder I have been working on," I said. "I call it Stinkarooni because it *really* stinks. It also creates smoke. It isn't perfected yet, but it might come in handy. Just in case." I put it in my pocket.

"Good idea," Mellie said.

"I hope we don't need it," Scotty replied.

We rode our bikes to the caves. The area still looked

peaceful and surrounded by nature. But this time, I felt an undercurrent of unease as we parked our bikes. We stopped at the entrance of the caves. Before, we were here to have fun. Now, we were on a mission to help Eleanor and Robert and, ultimately, ourselves.

"We have to find that diary," I said, knowing we all needed a little push.

"We know," Mellie replied.

"We wish we didn't," Scotty said, cleaning his glasses. "But how can we find it? This place is huge."

"And don't forget about those creatures," said Mellie.

"I didn't forget," I said. "We'll just have to be careful."

No one wanted to take the first step. Mellie looked around nervously, her eyes darting quickly in multiple directions. Scotty peered behind him, as if to see if he could find a fast getaway. I squared my shoulders, smiled at them, and said, "Come on. Let's go." We cautiously went into the caves together.

We had our flashlights but didn't need them when we entered. Nothing seemed unusual. The cave smelled damp. It was a little cool. Scotty pulled up the collar of his shirt.

We decided to take a different tunnel than we had before. We turned to take the tunnel on the right. The deeper we ventured into the caves, the darker it got. We didn't see or hear anything you wouldn't expect in a cave.

As the tunnel curved to the left, we saw cobwebs hanging from the ceiling. Some of them touched the tops of our heads and shoulders. Mellie was in front of us and walked into a thicker section of them.

"These cobwebs are really sticking to me," Mellie said with a shiver. "It feels like icy cold fingers are touching my scalp and grabbing onto my shoulders." She tried to wipe them away. Then she yelled out in panic, "They're squeezing me!"

Scotty and I rushed to help her. We pulled the webs off her. It was difficult, but we did it. The cobwebs were very sticky, and it felt like they were burning our fingers. They came off like strands of thin rope. There were red marks on her arms and neck, and on my and Scotty's hands.

"What are those?" Mellie asked, rubbing her arms and neck.

"I don't know," I said, "but they're stronger than normal cobwebs. They're more like silk ropes. But very coarse."

As I spoke, the hair on my arms and the nape of my neck rose. It felt like something or someone was watching us. I didn't say anything to the others. They were already on edge. I tried to shake the feeling off but couldn't.

We continued through the tunnel we were on. Scotty stopped and pointed to the wall of the cave. "Looks like the walls are shiny," he said. "Like bits of sparkling glass."

"Yeah," said Mellie as she went to take a closer look.

"Maybe they are diamonds, and we'll all be rich," Scotty said, smiling broadly.

"That would be great," said Mellie.

Mellie went to touch the wall. Then our excitement turned to horror. Something sharp grabbed Mellie's sleeve and pulled her slowly toward the wall! She frantically tried to yank and twist away. "It won't let go," she yelled. The more she struggled, the faster her arm went toward the wall. "It's trying to eat my arm!" she shrieked.

Scotty and I ran to help her. We grasped her arm and pulled. Whatever it was that had her wouldn't let go. Mellie made a fist to try to stop her hand from going into the wall. But it wasn't giving up. It still had a hold of her sleeve. She tried to yank her arm away from the wall again. When she did, whatever had her pulled her arm back to the wall. "It won't let go," Mellie screamed, panicked. Scotty and I tugged hard on her arm, too.

Suddenly, part of a sand-colored creature came out

of the wall. At first, I thought it resembled a maggot, but its body was about six inches long and thick. Its skin looked like sandpaper. It didn't have a head! The skin on the front of its body slid back, and all I could see were rows and rows of tiny razor-blade sharp teeth on the roof of its mouth. Its tongue was blood-stained and sharp, with black gooey saliva oozing off it. Its teeth were strangely shiny. I figured that the shininess attracted smaller insects and anything else that had the misfortune of coming too close. As it approached, its tongue slid out, skewered its prey, and brought it in. Its upper teeth bit down on it. Then it swallowed its prey whole, even if it wasn't dead yet.

"I think it's stronger than us," yelled Mellie. She let out a piercing scream in terror. Hearing that scared Scotty and me more than anything. We took a deep breath and tugged with all our might. We were able to prevent her hand from going into the wall and yanked her free.

Half of her sleeve was gone, but she was okay. The creature had gone back into the wall, eating her sleeve. We could hear the creature tearing and ripping it.

Another of these shiny teeth maggot creatures crept out of another hole in a different wall. It looked like it

was going to bite Scotty's shoulder. Before it could, I hit it with a rock. When that happened, the whole wall came alive with a screeching sound. It started low, then got higher and higher pitched and louder. We had to cover our ears.

Suddenly, these shiny teeth maggot creatures started sliding down the walls. Dozens of them were trying to get at us. They made a wet *plop* as they fell to the cave floor.

Some slid onto us, but we were able to push them off. One landed on Scotty's head. He howled in fright. I knocked it off.

"Hurry, that way!" I yelled, as I pointed to a tunnel on the right.

We flew through the tunnel. I could hear the wet, scraping, and sliding movements of the shiny teeth maggot creatures. I didn't know if we were running in the right direction to the entrance of the cave. After what seemed like forever, we came to an intersection. We could continue in the tunnel we were on or go right or left. We stopped to catch our breath.

"Which way?" yelled Scotty.

"I don't know," I gasped. "Listen." The wet, scraping, and sliding noises drew closer.

"The sound seems to be coming from all three tunnels," Mellie shouted.

"Oh, no," Scotty wailed. "We're trapped!"

"Wait a second," I said. "I think it's just echoing through the other two tunnels."

"But which one should we take?" Scotty hollered, ready to take off, almost running in place.

I pointed to the tunnel we were in. "This one. I think."

"You *'think'*?" Scotty yelled, pulling his glasses off.

I grabbed him and Mellie by the arm. "C'mon, this way." I had my fingers crossed.

CHAPTER 12

We ran through the tunnel. With our flashlights on, there was just enough light for us to see. Up ahead, it was dark. But, in the distance, we saw a faint glow.

"What is that?" asked Mellie.

"Maybe it's a way out," Scotty said hopefully.

"Stop," I yelled. "It's the creatures! I can hear them. And they're coming towards us. Turn off your flashlights."

"We're trapped!" howled Scotty.

I hastily looked around. My eyes adjusted quickly, just enough to see an opening to our right. It was still a little ways away.

"Maybe we could hide there," I said. It wasn't very

big, but it was big enough for all three of us to fit. Mellie and Scotty saw the opening as well.

"Follow me. Stay quiet," I whispered. We couldn't see very well and didn't want to turn on our flashlights. "Hold on to each other."

Mellie clutched my shirt. Scotty grabbed Mellie's shirt. I felt my way along the cave wall. The sounds of the creatures advancing, scraping, and sliding through the tunnel drew closer.

Scotty kept looking behind him. "If they find us, I'll be their first meal," he whispered in fear.

Mellie turned her head and whispered, "I'll be their second. Shhhhhh."

We finally got to the opening in the wall. It was a crevice, just big enough for all three of us to hide in. I put my arm out to feel my way, hoping there was nothing in there that would bite me. Mellie and Scotty followed me in.

"This should hide us until the creatures pass," I said softly, with more confidence than I was actually feeling.

"Hopefully, they won't know we're here and will quickly pass us by," Mellie whispered nervously.

"*If* they pass us," Scotty moaned softly.

We knew we couldn't go back for fear of meeting up

with the creatures. If we were found now, for sure, we would be trapped.

I wanted to give Mellie and Scotty a little hope. I quietly breathed out, "It'll be all right."

We huddled together. Our backs were against the wall. Again. We made ourselves as small as we could.

"I can't look," whispered Scotty. He clutched Mellie's arm. Mellie grasped my arm.

I could hear the creatures were very close. The creatures were almost at the crevice. We held on tighter to each other, holding our breath, afraid to breathe. We were frozen in fear of being found. It seemed that time was suspended.

Then we could hear that wet, scraping, sliding sound as the creatures passed the crevice. It seemed like it took forever for the creatures to go by.

We started to breathe again. We would be okay.

Then Scotty made a slight wheezing sound. I quickly turned to him. Before I could do anything, he sneezed. He looked at Mellie and me in horror. We stared at each other, hoping the creatures didn't hear it.

At first, we didn't hear anything. Scotty and Mellie looked relieved. The creatures had kept going. Then I heard that dreadful scraping and sliding sound. The maggot creatures were coming back toward us!

"Oh, no, now what?" asked Mellie frantically.

I could hear the creatures creeping closer. They stopped in front of the crevice. They were almost upon us. My mind raced to think about what we should do.

"Ollie! Your Stinkarooni powder," Scotty screamed. "Now would be a good time to use it!"

"Good thinking." As I tried to pull it out of my pocket, the bag fell to the ground. The creatures were right in front of us.

"Hurry!" Mellie shrieked.

"Ollie, they're going to get us," yelled Scotty.

When the bag fell, it had opened a little. That was lucky for me, I didn't have to open it. I quickly scooped it up and threw it in the path of the maggot creatures.

"Ewww," Mellie groaned. "You weren't kidding . . . Stinkarooni! It smells worse than a porta potty on a hot day at the summer fair."

"I think I'm going to puke," Scotty gagged.

When they came into contact with the putrid Stinkarooni stench, the creatures instantly stopped.

"I think it's working!" I yelled.

The creatures scurried away as fast as they could. They shrieked so loud and hideously that Mellie,

Scotty, and I almost screamed. That dreadful scraping and sliding sound actually sounded good to us as it got further away. Within a few minutes, the creatures disappeared. I didn't know where they went, but I was glad they were gone!

We took a collective deep breath.

"That was close," said Mellie.

"I hoped if they got me, they would get sick and choke!" Scotty joked. We all laughed at that.

"It's okay now," I said, trying to be reassuring. "It sounds like they're gone. We can turn our flashlights on again."

We tentatively turned on our flashlights, still fearful that some of the creatures might still be nearby. But they were gone. I could only see the floor and walls of the cave.

"The coast seems clear," I said. "Let's go." As I shined my light around, something caught my eye. A cloth sticking out from the dirt in a corner of the crevice.

I stepped toward it to get a better look. "What is that?" Mellie asked

"Who cares?" Scotty said. "I think we should go now."

"I don't know," I said. "It seems familiar somehow. I just want to get a quick look." I picked it up, but part of it was buried. I got on my hands and knees and started digging around it to loosen the dirt.

"It looks like it's just an old handkerchief," said Mellie. "Scotty is right. We should try and get out of here."

"Yeah, before those creatures find us again," Scotty said.

"Okay, just one second." I dug faster. When I thought I had uncovered it enough, I tried to pull it up. It was still a little stuck, so I tugged harder. I could tell I almost had it loose. Then we saw a light under the cloth.

"Oh, no, it's those creatures!" Scotty yelled.

"Ollie, let's go," Mellie pleaded, trying to pull me up. I was getting ready to get up and run when I saw something.

"No, I think it's okay," I said. "It's a soft white light. It's not the creatures." The cloth was wrapped around something. I jerked the cloth to try to loosen it from the ground. It worked. I reached down to pull up the rest of the cloth and whatever it was covering. I lifted off the cloth. I was shocked at what I saw.

"What is that?" asked Scotty anxiously. "It looks like a book."

It did look like a book with an old leather cover. A large script "E" was embossed on the front cover. And it glowed in my hands.

"That's not a book," Mellie exclaimed.

"It's a diary!" I shouted. I raised it in the air. Then, remembering the creatures, I whispered, "We found Eleanor's diary!"

CHAPTER 13

I gave the diary, wrapped in the handkerchief, to Scotty. He took it like he thought it might bite him and put it in the backpack. I looked around, trying to figure out the best way to get out of the cave. I pointed to the tunnel I thought would be the way to go. "That way," I said.

We rushed back through the tunnel. Every once in a while, we thought we heard something. We'd stop and listen. Then all was quiet again. Finally, we found the entrance. We were relieved and ran to our bikes.

We stopped dead in our tracks. Something didn't look right. We stared at our bikes. They were entwined together with some sticky, coarse rope.

"What is this now?" Scotty asked, frowning.

"Looks like the same cobweb-type rope we saw earlier in the cave," said Mellie. She rubbed her neck and shoulders.

I examined the bikes. "It is. It's the same stuff," I said.

We tried to wipe it off with our hands, but it stuck to and burned our hands again, leaving marks. When we wiped our hands on our clothes, it clung to our clothes and left burn marks.

"This is getting us nowhere," I said in frustration. Then I remembered the handkerchief around the diary. "Scotty, pull out that handkerchief that we found the diary wrapped in," I said.

Scotty, understanding my intention, tried using the handkerchief to remove the rope from his bike. The rope slid off easily, as if it were trying to get away from the cloth.

But when Mellie or I tried to use the handkerchief to wipe off the rope, it didn't come off. It still clung to the bike.

"The handkerchief seems to only work for you, Scotty," I said. Mellie nodded.

Scotty shrugged. "I don't know why it works for me, but I'm glad it does so we can get out of here." When he finished wiping off our bikes, we quickly rode to our cabin.

Once we got back, we discussed our close call with the creatures.

"That was the second encounter with strange, creepy creatures," Mellie said.

"I know," Scotty said, as he cleaned his glasses. "Both encounters could have ended badly for us. I'll never forget that scraping, sliding sound. I'm going to have nightmares because of them."

"One encounter was bad enough," I said. "But two? I don't think what happened to us was a coincidence."

"What do you mean?" asked Scotty.

"I know there are creatures in caves that we wouldn't normally see," I said. "But if creatures like this attacked other people, I think someone would have reported it."

"Maybe there have been attacks, but no one knew what happened to the people attacked," Mellie suggested.

"Yeah," Scotty said. "Maybe there was never any proof of the attacks on other people."

"That could all be true, but I don't think so," I said.

Mellie and Scotty looked at me. Expectantly, waiting for me to continue.

"I'm sure that Victor was behind the attacks," I continued. "Remember, Old Henry told us Victor was involved in black magic? In both attacks, the creatures seemed to be after us. Victor wants us out of the way."

"That's even worse," sighed Scotty.

"If he can do that, who knows what else he has in store for us," Mellie speculated.

"We have to find some way to help Eleanor and Robert and end this curse . . . soon," I said.

"But how?" asked Scotty.

"Well, Eleanor told us to find the diary. We did. Let's start there," I said.

"Yes, maybe we can find the information we need in it," Mellie said.

"Scotty, pass me the diary," I said.

Scotty pulled the book out of the backpack and gave it to me. When I touched it, the diary started glowing again. I had forgotten about that. I almost dropped it out of fear. Then something told me it was all right. I don't know why, but I wasn't scared of it. It felt warm and comforting in my hand.

We sat at the table, and I was looking at Eleanor's diary when a thought occurred to me.

"Mellie, open the diary," I said.

Mellie looked at me perplexed. "Why don't you want to open it?" she asked.

"I will, but I'm checking out a theory I have." I placed the diary in front of her.

She picked it up and turned it over. "It doesn't look to have a lock on it," she said.

"It doesn't glow when Mellie holds it," Scotty observed. I nodded.

"Well, let's see what's inside," said Mellie. She tried to open the cover but couldn't. The page wouldn't turn. Then she attempted to open it from the middle. But it wouldn't open at all. She looked at Scotty and me, surprised that she couldn't open it.

"Scotty, you try and open it," I said.

Scotty picked up the diary. It didn't glow. We hadn't noticed that before when he handed it to me. He tried to open it, but he wasn't able to. It remained closed.

"I can't open it either," Scotty said.

"Okay, my turn." As soon as I touched the diary, it started glowing again. I was feeling more confident. I looked at Mellie and Scotty in anticipation.

"I have a feeling I can open it." I waited a moment, then asked, "Are we ready for this?" Mellie and Scotty nodded, surprised at the turn of events.

"Okay, here we go." I carefully tried to lift the cover. For one second, it wouldn't open. I held my breath. Maybe it wouldn't open for me either. I tried again. I rubbed my hands together, hoping that would help in some way. I was willing to try anything. I lifted the cover slowly. It turned easily in my fingers. I barely had to turn it.

Eleanor's diary opened.

CHAPTER 14

I was excited about reading the diary. The paper was old and yellow. The handwriting was well-formed and flowed smoothly. I read aloud about Eleanor being in love with Robert. She wrote about their future plans of being together and how their lives would be, happy with each other.

A few pages in, Eleanor wrote about Victor. How handsome and rich he was. She wrote of his interest in her. At first, she had been flattered, but she was only interested in Robert, her true love. She tried to discourage Victor, but that made him want her all the more.

At this point, I noted, "Eleanor's handwriting has started to change. It's more erratic and stilted." I speculated that she was upset as she wrote down her thoughts. It was as if she were hurried.

"Eleanor wrote that Victor started to get angry with her," I continued. "She tried to gently explain to him that she was only interested in Robert. That made Victor angrier. He would grab Eleanor by the shoulders and shake her or roughly grab her arms and squeeze until she pleaded for him to release her. He made sure not to leave marks where anyone would see them.

"Eleanor tried to tell her family and friends about Victor's aggression, but they thought she should be happy with his attention. They thought she was exaggerating his anger.

"Victor began to threaten Eleanor, saying that if he couldn't have her, no one else would. He threatened to hurt Robert. The paper is a little wrinkled here," I noted. "I wonder if she was crying when she wrote this."

Mellie and Scotty looked at me sadly and nodded.

I continued, "Eleanor didn't dare tell Robert, fearing that he would confront Victor. She didn't know what to do. She decided to make plans to get away from Victor. She thought they would be safe if they could sneak away without Victor finding out."

I stopped there. Mellie and Scotty were looking at

me expectantly.

"Keep going," Mellie said.

"Yeah. Don't keep us hanging," Scotty pleaded. "What happened next?"

"Well . . . we saw that movie-like reenactment in the picture," I said sadly. "So, we know what happened that night."

The room was deathly silent.

"What a tragic story," said Mellie.

"Victor said that anyone who tried to help them would be destroyed," Scotty said nervously.

"Other people and creatures have tried to destroy us before," I replied.

"I wish you hadn't said that," said Scotty.

"We still have to help Eleanor and Robert," said Mellie.

All three of us sat silently for a few minutes. Then I stretched my arm out on the table. Mellie put her arm out, too. After a brief hesitation, so did Scotty. We bumped fists.

"Friends Forever," we said together, smiling.

CHAPTER 15

A few hours later, I felt more determined than ever. "Let's go over what we have," I said. "The diary tells us the story and supposedly gives clues for breaking the curse. We haven't gone through it totally yet."

I read again from the diary. "You can't continue until you solve this:

"Look not within but without.
What is there is not the same.
Find the tear. That is your aim.
Find my love so there is no doubt."

"What does that mean?" asked Scotty.

"I don't know." I tried to turn the page. "It won't turn," I said.

"I guess we have to figure it out before we can move on," said Mellie.

We decided to go back to Eleanor's house to see if we could find some clues to help us solve the riddle.

Before leaving, Mellie said, "Wait a second. I just thought of something." She brought out the amulet from her room. "I don't know if we'll need this, but I'll feel better if we have it with us."

"Great idea," I said.

"We need all the help we can get," said Scotty.

As we cycled along the trail toward Eleanor's house, her words were going around and around in my brain. *Look not within but without.* It must be outside the house, I thought. *What is there is not the same.*

When we reached the house, we looked around. Like before, we saw trees and bushes. We strode around the house. We didn't see anything that stood out. Then I remembered the first time I perused the area with the rotting tree limbs sticking out of the ground . . . like they were reaching out of the ground.

"Before, when we came here, I had a funny feeling that I was being pushed to notice or study this area," I recalled. "I didn't think too much about it. Now, though, I think we should take a closer look."

We walked to the area. "Just some decaying tree limbs," Scotty observed.

"Not much here to see," Mellie said.

"There's something here," I replied. "There must be. Otherwise, Eleanor wouldn't have mentioned it. Keep checking."

We started inspecting closer to the tree limbs in the ground. Scotty was scrutinizing the area. He backed up into one of the limbs.

"Yuck," he said. He moved his hand. It was wet.

"What happened?" I asked.

"I'm not sure," Scotty said. "I backed up into one of these limbs, and it's all wet."

"Let me see," said Mellie. She examined Scotty's hand. Sure enough, there were droplets of what looked like sap on his hand, but it was wetter.

"Check this out," I said. I closely examined the limb Scotty bumped into. It was completely covered with hundreds, maybe thousands of droplets.

"The limb is coated with droplets," Mellie said.

"But look at the shape of them," I said.

"What shape is that?" asked Mellie.

"They aren't circular. They're kind of oblong. That's weird," Scotty observed.

"Like the shape of tears?" I asked.

"What? Whose tears?" asked Scotty.

"Think about what Eleanor instructed us to do:

'Find the tear that is your aim.
Find my love so there is no doubt.'"

"Now, remember what Victor said when we saw the scene in the picture," I said. "Robert would always be close, but always apart. These are Robert's tears," I exclaimed. "*This is Robert!*"

CHAPTER 16

After finding what we thought might be Robert, we all backed up. Mellie and Scotty looked shocked. Mellie's hand covered her mouth.

"Poor Robert," she said.

Scotty shook his head and said sadly, "No wonder no one knew what happened to him."

I repeated the rhyme out loud:

"Look not within but without
What is there is not the same
Find the tear that is your aim
Find my love so there is no doubt.

"That sounds about right," I speculated. "This is what happened to Robert after Victor put a curse on him. He is near but can't help Eleanor. He can hear Eleanor sighing and crying but can't do anything about it."

"We'll have to see if we are right," I continued. "We'll know we are right if I can turn the page in the diary. Let's go back and see."

As we headed back toward our bikes, Mellie stopped.

"What's wrong?" I asked.

"Did you feel that?" she asked.

"No," I said as I scanned the area.

"Feel what?" asked Scotty.

The ground started to tremble, then stopped. We looked around. Nothing seemed out of place. Then the trembling began again. The ground we were standing on was shaking.

"What is that?" I asked.

Before Mellie and Scotty could answer me, the shaking increased. It knocked over our bikes. The trembling increased so much that we had to hang on to each other for support, or was it in fear? I wasn't sure.

The next thing I knew, I was on the ground. It looked like the surface of the ground was moving. I couldn't quite make out what was happening.

Then up from the ground came hundreds and hundreds of roaches. Or what looked like roaches. They had the body of roaches but the many legs of a centipede. And they were big—some about five inches long. Others were longer. And they were coming right for us!

"Run!" I yelled.

I didn't have to worry about that. Mellie and Scotty were already racing ahead of me. The roaches blocked the way to our bikes. Mellie and Scotty were running toward Eleanor's house.

"No, not that way!" I yelled, afraid of what we might find in the house. "Head for the caves!"

We quickly changed direction. We ran faster than ever, but the roaches were catching up to us. The ground trembled harder beneath our feet.

Scotty looked back and shrieked, "They're gaining on us."

Sure enough, the roaches were closing the distance between us. We could hear them gnashing and shuffling. It was loud and close.

"Ollie!" Mellie screamed as a roach jumped, almost touching her heel.

I grabbed Mellie's arm and pulled her faster ahead. "We're almost there," I yelled, even though we still had a

ways to go. I didn't know what we would do once we got there. The roaches could follow us into the cave. Then I remembered the amulet.

"Mellie, use the amulet," I hollered.

"How?" she screamed.

"Try anything," Scotty bellowed. "But do it fast."

Mellie grabbed the amulet from her pocket and pressed on the jewel. "Please work, please work," she kept saying. Nothing happened. We were running as fast as we could, and the roaches were almost upon us. "Oh, no," she shouted.

"We've had it now," Scotty shouted.

Suddenly, we felt a rush of warm air around us. To our amazement, the trees near us bent over the path. Their movements were smooth and deliberate. I didn't hear a sound. The branches lay across the path. We slowed down, not knowing what was going on. Afraid this was another threat. We were scared.

Then I understood what was happening.

"Grab on. Hold tight," I hollered.

Each of us climbed onto a branch. As we did, the branches seemed to encircle us, almost cradling us. Then the trees gently lifted us to safety. Mellie and Scotty closed their eyes.

"Thank you, thank you," Mellie kept mumbling.

"Help us, help us. Higher. Higher," Scotty was praying.

The trees lifted us out of harm's way and hid us high in the trees, away from the roach-like creatures. It all happened in a matter of seconds. Barely enough time, as the creatures approached and continued past us, leaving Mellie, Scotty, and me in shock and wonderment. But safe.

After a while, the trees gently lowered us to the ground. As we gratefully started to make our way back to our bikes, I turned around. One of the limbs seemed to sway back and forth, as if to say goodbye.

But that couldn't be, I thought. *Could it?*

We got back to our bikes without incident and rode back to our cabin.

CHAPTER 17

The following day, when we got up, Uncle John was already gone. He left a note on the table saying he wouldn't be back until late.

The first thing Mellie, Scotty, and I talked about were the trees and the roach creatures.

"I can't believe the trees saved us," said Mellie.

"I can't believe it either," said Scotty. "And what about those roach creatures? I didn't think we were going to make it."

"I know what you mean," I said. "If it wasn't for the amulet, I don't know if we would have made it to safety. Thank goodness you had it with you."

"I pushed on the jewel again when the creatures

were gone," said Mellie. "The trees put us down. I don't know why it worked for me, but I'm glad it did."

"Me too!" said Scotty.

"Let's see if we were right about the rotting tree limb covered with wet tears being Robert," I said. "I have a feeling it is. Otherwise, I don't think those roach creatures would have come after us. We're helping Eleanor little by little, and Victor is trying to stop us."

I pulled Eleanor's diary out of the desk drawer where I had put it the last time we read it. I opened it to the last page I had read. I grasped the corner of the next page, took a breath, and tried to turn the page.

At first, the page wouldn't turn. I looked at Mellie and Scotty, confused and concerned. I tried again, being careful not to damage it in some way. Then the page seemed to slip between my fingers and turn on its own. I smiled with a sigh of relief.

"That's good," Mellie said.

"At least we're on the right track," Scotty agreed.

"Let's see what Eleanor has to say next," I replied.

I read from Eleanor's diary and told Mellie and Scotty what it said. "Eleanor feels that she and Robert are in danger. She fears Victor won't stop until she is his. She is so afraid. She wants to take some measures so that if something happens to her, it will be known what happened."

"That was smart of her," Mellie said.

I continued to read. "Eleanor knew what Victor was capable of. She knew that if something happened to Robert, no one would be able to help her. Eleanor thought that if she put some clues in her diary, maybe someone could help her if they found it. But she hoped it would never come to that."

"Unfortunately, it did," Scotty said sadly.

I nodded. "When Eleanor was a child, her grandmother had told her she didn't have much to give her, but she did have two important things. Her grandmother told her about the amulet.

"Her grandmother said the amulet had special powers. But it would only respond to certain people. The special powers come from a combination of the amulet's power and that person's virtue. It could be used for good or evil. Her grandmother said it may help Eleanor if she were ever in danger. She said to always keep it hidden and safe. That it might protect her someday."

I turned the page and continued, "Eleanor's grandmother also gave her a handkerchief. She said to keep it with her, mentioning that it also had special powers that might help her someday as well. Eleanor didn't understand what her grandmother was telling her at the time. She just thought it was a keepsake from her grandmother. But she kept it with her always."

I stopped reading. "That must be the handkerchief we found wrapped around the diary."

"Things are becoming a little bit clearer," said Mellie.

"Not really," said Scotty, scratching his head.

I returned to the diary and continued with what Eleanor wrote. "As time passed, and once her grandmother died, Eleanor forgot about the amulet. Her life had turned out very well. She was in love with Robert and thought they would be happy forever. And then Victor showed up."

"Now, instead of happy forever, she is cursed forever," said Mellie.

I looked up and nodded. I knew what she meant. "She wasn't sure what to do about her situation with Victor. Then she came up with an idea—maybe the amulet could help her somehow.

"Her grandmother had said that the amulet would only respond to certain individuals. Eleanor had found instructions on how to use the amulet among her grandmother's possessions. So, using the amulet's power,

Eleanor made it so the diary and handkerchief would only respond to certain people, increasing their power as well. They would only work for those who are exceptional.

"Eleanor also wrote that those who could help her break the curse must fit the following:

'One who is knowledgeable.
One who has a logical and feminine heart.
One who is courageous but whose courage is hidden.'"

Mellie, Scotty, and I looked at each other, in understanding. "That could be us," I said. "Now we know why this diary, the amulet, and the handkerchief respond to each of us. We are the ones who can help her."

"But what is exceptional about us?" Scotty asked.

"I don't know," I said. I tried to turn the page but couldn't. "That's as far as we can go for now," I said. "Looks like it's back to Eleanor's house."

CHAPTER 18

We knew we needed to return to Eleanor's house, but nobody seemed enthusiastic about it. Scotty looked at me, took off his glasses, and cleaned them. Mellie played with her hair and nodded, but it didn't look like she wanted to go.

"We have to see if there are any more clues that will help us," I said. "Maybe we can contact Eleanor somehow to find out what else we need to know. The solution to all of this starts in that house."

"I'll put the amulet on so it doesn't get lost and so Eleanor can see that we have it," said Mellie. She secured it around her neck.

Scotty reluctantly grabbed the handkerchief and put

it in his pocket. "Just in case," he said meekly.

We rode our bikes to Eleanor's house. As we approached the building, something didn't seem right.

"The house looks a little weird," said Mellie.

"Yeah, I'm not sure what—" I started to say.

"It looks like it's breathing," interrupted Scotty.

We all stopped in our tracks and stared at the house. Sure enough, it looked like the house walls were pulsing in and out. It was very strange looking and was terrifying. A wheezing sound emanated from the house.

"It must be an illusion created by Victor," I said. "He just wants to scare us off."

"He's doing a good job," said Scotty.

Mellie nodded in agreement.

"Let's show him we're not scared easily," I said.

"You show him," said Scotty as he turned to run away.

Mellie grabbed the back of his shirt and pulled him back. "We stay together," she said. "Scotty does have a point, Ollie," she continued as she stared at the house.

"I know, but . . ." I didn't finish my sentence. It seemed the breathing or pulsing had stopped. "C'mon," I said as I walked toward the house.

"Maybe it was our imagination," said Mellie.

"Not mine," Scotty retorted, as he reluctantly

followed me.

"I guess we'll go through the front door," I said. "It's a little late to try and sneak in. Victor obviously knows we're here."

"Good reason to get out of here," mumbled Scotty.

I stopped abruptly in my tracks as we approached the front door. A feeling of dread came over me. I then remembered Eleanor and Robert and why we were there in the first place.

I tentatively touched the doorknob. Nothing happened. There was no sharp pain or anything unusual. With determination, I quickly grabbed and turned it. Once again, there were no unusual feelings. With a sigh of relief, I opened the door and stepped into the house. Scotty pushed Mellie in.

"Stop that," she said as she reached to swat his hand.

Scotty gave a small laugh and followed her in. We slowly made our way to the living room and gazed around.

"What are we looking for again?" asked Scotty, his eyes darting around nervously.

"I don't know," I said. "I was hoping we could find some answers here. Spread out and see if there might be anything else that may help us."

Suddenly, Mellie fell forward. "Quit pushing me, Scotty." She turned around, but Scotty was across the room.

"What did you say, Mellie?" he asked, looking at her curiously.

"Nothing," she said. "I must have tripped over something. Must be my nerves." She rubbed her shoulder. "My shoulder feels cold and sore," she stated.

She turned toward us and gasped. "It wasn't my nerves," Mellie said.

CHAPTER 19

Scotty and I turned to Mellie to see what was wrong. Out of nowhere, the figure of a man appeared. He was standing just a few feet away from Scotty and me. I could only stare at him. I could see through him, but his image was still very clear. I blinked a few times to ensure I was actually seeing him. Unfortunately, I was.

"Whoa," yelped Scotty as he jumped back.

Surprised, I jumped back also, almost knocking into Scotty.

It was Victor! The anger and hatred on his face now marred the handsomeness that once was there.

"I will destroy you now," he roared. He took a step toward Scotty and me. His fingers curled like sharp animal claws. Ready to strike.

"Leave them alone," yelled Mellie.

Victor immediately turned to her. And then he stared at the amulet around her neck. He smiled evilly and said, "I will take care of you first." He lunged at Mellie.

She backed up, but her back was against a chair. She looked like she didn't know what to do. It all happened so fast. Victor was in front of her before she knew it. He reached for her. His clawed fingers were going for her neck.

"He's going to choke her!" Scotty yelled. "Stay away from her!" He took a step to help Mellie.

Mellie then realized Victor was going for the amulet around her neck.

Victor reached for it. As soon as his hands got close to the amulet, blue sparks exploded from it and surrounded his hands, turning them black. Victor stepped back and yelled in pain and frustration. He backed up and stared at all three of us with pure hatred in his eyes. His eyes were glowing red. I wouldn't have been surprised if flames flew out of them. He raised his arms. *Uh oh*, I thought, thinking that might actually happen. Instead, a lightning bolt hit the wall near us, leaving a strong burning stench that filled the room. Our hair stood on end. Suddenly, Victor disappeared.

"What happened?" asked Scotty.

Mellie stood in place, trembling. Scotty and I went to comfort her.

"We must be close to finding something or knowing something important for him to show himself like that," I reasoned.

"He wanted this amulet," Mellie said. She touched the amulet with her finger, her hand shaking as she did. Then she pushed her hair out of her eyes.

"Eleanor's grandmother told her that the amulet was powerful," I said. "It must be. It stopped Victor from taking it."

"Why did he want it?" asked Scotty.

"He must know that it could hurt him or stop the curse somehow," I said.

"I think we've had enough excitement for one day," said Scotty. "Let's get out of here." He was inching his way toward the doorway.

"Mellie, are you okay?" I asked.

Mellie looked at us. Her face seemed to show some relief, but her hands were still shaking. "I'm okay now," she said. "I just wasn't expecting that to happen. That was very brave of you, Scotty, to try to come to help me.

What were you going to do?"

"I wish I knew." Scotty shrugged with an embarrassed smile. "I was hoping something would come to me."

"I know we're all shaken up," I said. "But we should stay a little longer to see if we can find anything that might help us."

"I wish you'd quit saying that," said Scotty. "Okay, but just for a little while."

We went from room to room. We didn't find anything that might be helpful. We were nervous, always looking over our shoulders for fear that Victor would reappear. But he didn't.

After a while, we started to relax a bit. I saw Scotty go into the bedroom. Something must have caught his attention because I heard him ask, "What was that?" The next thing I knew, he screamed. We ran to see what was wrong.

We rushed into the bedroom. Scotty wasn't there. We sprinted into the next room.

"He must be in here," I said.

We quickly looked around. But Scotty was nowhere to be seen.

Suddenly, we heard Scotty yell, "Help, help, help!" We sped back into the bedroom. We looked in every direction. We couldn't see him.

"Ollie! Mellie! Help me!" Scotty pleaded. The sound was coming from the wall. We realized Scotty was in the wall!

We tried to follow his voice. We could hear his feet pounding on the floor.

"Scotty, where are you?" I yelled out.

"Hurry!" Scotty screamed. "There's someone or something in here with me. It's trying to grab me! Heeelp meee . . ." His voice was starting to fade.

"Oh, no, Ollie, we have to find him!" Mellie screamed in panic.

As we ran along the wall, trying to find Scotty, a hand grabbed my shoulder! I shouted out in fear.

"Ollie," Scotty yelled, "it's me."

I grabbed Scotty's hand and pulled. "Mellie, help!" I shouted. Mellie saw what was happening and ran to help. We tugged hard on Scotty's arm, but we couldn't free him from the wall. We yanked with all our might. For a moment, it seemed like Scotty's arm was slipping from our grasp. We clenched even tighter.

"Don't let go," I screamed. Finally, when we were almost out of strength and our muscles were about to give out, we pulled Scotty out of the wall. We all landed on the floor. Breathing hard. We were unable to believe what had just occurred.

Scotty looked at Mellie and me. "Thanks," he breathed out.

"What happened?" I asked.

"I went into the bedroom," Scotty replied. "I thought I saw something. I quickly turned my head. I saw a whisp of dark mist disappear where two walls connected. I went to the wall. I carefully touched where I thought I saw the dark mist disappear. Suddenly, I was pulled into the wall!"

"How did you find the opening to get out?" I asked.

"I didn't," Scotty whispered. "*Someone or something* pushed me out."

We all looked at each other in shock and disbelief.

Suddenly, we heard Eleanor's voice. "You must go quickly. You are in more danger than you know. You are the ones who can break the curse. Read the diary. Find the answers you need to put an end to this evil deed."

For a moment, we were quiet. Then Scotty asked, "Can we go now?"

CHAPTER 20

Back in our cabin, I took out Eleanor's diary. I was able to turn the page.

I read from the diary, "Eleanor feared that the possibility of anyone helping her was very low. But at the same time, she hoped someone would be able to, by some miracle.

"Eleanor hated what Victor did to her and Robert. 'Robert, Robert!' She sobbed his name over and over. She swore she would do everything she could to break the curse.

"She wrote, 'If you have gotten this far, there is hope in my heart. You must be the ones who can help me. *Please, please* help me. There is nowhere else I can turn.'"

I stopped.

"Once again, the page is wrinkled," I said.

"With her tears," Mellie sighed.

Scotty sniffed and nodded.

After a few moments, I continued reading. "To break this curse, you will need:

"Something made of evil,
Tears within and tears without,
The smoke of needles, and
A possession of Victor's.

"Remember this, these cannot be used without a possession of his. You need something of Victor's to complete the deed. Once you have everything, you must say these words:

Eleanor and Robert's love was true
It is now time for them to start anew
Break this curse that holds them tight
Let our love be strong to release them
So their love can again shine bright."

I glanced at Mellie and Scotty. I could tell they were

trying to figure it all out. Mellie looked like she was going over every detail in her mind. Scotty was staring at me as if hoping the answers would suddenly reveal themselves to him.

I continued reading, "All of these are needed to break the curse. Most importantly, the goodness of your spirit and love for each other is essential. Otherwise, all is for naught. You must succeed . . . for Robert, for me, and for yourselves.

"Be forewarned, if you fail to destroy Victor, he will do everything in his power to destroy you, or worse, lock your spirits in this house forever—never to be seen again!"

CHAPTER 21

"That's it," I said. I closed the diary.

"Wow," said Mellie, looking overwhelmed.

"How are we going to do all of that?" asked Scotty. "I didn't even understand all of it."

"I know what you mean," I said. "We'll just have to figure it out, somehow. Let's go through each one and see what we have."

"Okay," said Mellie. "We need *something made of evil.* Like what?"

We all thought about it. After a few minutes, no one said anything.

"Any ideas?" I asked.

"Not really," said Mellie. "Everything about Victor is

evil. But we don't know of anything Victor made."

"Victor is made of evil," Scotty said. "But that doesn't really seem to fit."

"I think you both might be on to something," I said hopefully.

Scotty and Mellie looked at me, confused. "What do you mean?" asked Scotty. He scratched his head.

"Victor is made of evil," I said. "*Something made of evil*. It must be something Victor made. I think we might know of something Victor made."

Mellie and Scotty tried to make sense of it. "Something Victor made . . ." Scotty said, as he stared into space, trying to put the pieces together.

Mellie's eyes suddenly got bigger. "You don't mean the creatures, do you?" she exclaimed.

"That's exactly what I mean," I said. "Victor practiced black magic. The creatures coming after us . . . we all felt they were coming to get us. I think Victor made those creatures."

"I think you're right," said Mellie. "It makes sense."

"So, what are you saying?" Scotty asked, taking off his glasses, looking worried. "We need those creatures to end the curse?" He gulped loudly.

"Not all of them," I said. "One should do it. At least,

I hope so."

"How are we even going to get one of the creatures?" asked Scotty, a touch of panic in his voice. "I don't want to go looking for them. No way."

I smiled. "We don't have to," I said. "You have one, Scotty."

"What?" Scotty asked, confused.

"Lift up your shoe," I said.

CHAPTER 22

Sure enough, under Scotty's shoe were the remnants of the maggot creature that had tried to bite him. Much of the creature, even though it was crushed, could still be seen on the sole. The creature's stickiness kept the body stuck to his shoe.

"We need to scrape it off and put it somewhere safe," I said.

"I'll get you a stick from outside," said Mellie.

Scotty nodded. As he was scraping it off, he said, "Yuck." He looked around, trying to find something to put it in. He spotted my old mixing bowl on the counter that I brought from home. There was a lion and a shield imprinted on the bowl. They had faded quite a bit. "Can

I just use this?" he asked.

"Sure," I said. "That's a good idea. We'll use it to mix everything up."

Scotty scraped as much of the creature off as he could and put it in the bowl.

When he was done, I said, "Okay, let's see what's next. Eleanor had written, *'Tears within and tears without.'* Any ideas what that could be?"

Mellie and Scotty thought about it for a while.

"Tears within what and tears without what?" asked Mellie. "I'm not sure. Eleanor cried a lot after what happened, but tears within what? Did she mean tears within her heart? I don't know."

"The only tears I can think of was the sap from the rotted tree limb," Scotty suggested. "The rotted tree limb we think is Robert. The sap was wet and shaped like tears."

"That could be it," I said. "The tears without could mean outside the house. And tears within might mean tears inside the house. I think we may have part of what Eleanor was trying to tell us. Next, she mentioned *the smoke of needles.* Any ideas?"

Mellie lifted her head and was lost in thought. Scotty looked down and shook his head, as if canceling out the ideas he was considering. I tapped on the table, trying to understand Eleanor's message.

After a while, I said, "I don't know. I keep thinking, what kind of needles smoke? Metal needles, like pins? But they don't smoke . . . *the smoke of needles*?" I shook my head.

Mellie and Scotty were quiet. They didn't have any ideas.

"We'll have to come back to that one," I said. "So far, we're not doing that great. After the needles, Eleanor wrote about needing *a possession of Victor's*."

"Where would we even find a possession of Victor's?" asked Scotty. "We certainly can't ask him for one."

We all laughed at that.

"A possession. Could that mean one of the creatures?" Mellie suggested.

"I only had the one, and I didn't want that one," said Scotty.

We all chuckled. I thought about it.

"I think there's more to it than the creatures," I said. "What, though? I don't know. But the last part about the goodness of spirit and love will be up to us."

"Eleanor wrote a lot. We only understand a little of it," Mellie said. "How are we going to figure the rest out?"

"We'll figure it out, somehow," I said. "We have to go back to Eleanor's house to see what we can find."

"I wish we could find something good for once," Scotty said. "How come there are always scary things? Maybe we should wait until tomorrow."

I patted Scotty's shoulder for encouragement. We slowly cycled our way back to Eleanor's house. I knew that we could find some answers there. Eleanor had written what was needed to destroy Victor. At least now we had some direction.

CHAPTER 23

We parked our bikes in front of Eleanor's house. I knew we had to come here, but not knowing what to expect, I was concerned about going back into the house. I looked at Mellie and Scotty. Mellie played with her hair and stroked her arms, as if to rub away chills. Scotty kept touching his glasses and looking around. I knew they were concerned, too.

As we approached the house, I decided to stop at the rotted tree limb. "We figured out that we need Robert's tears or the sap on the tree," I said. "Let's take a piece of the bark with tears on it. At least we'll have that part."

Scotty took out his knife and gently cut off a piece of bark with sap on it. "I hope I didn't hurt him," he said, frowning. His hand shook a little.

Mellie touched his arm. "Robert has been in pain from what happened all those years ago. He'll thank us when we help him." Scotty put the piece of bark in the backpack.

We cautiously walked up the steps and stopped, not wanting to go in. Worried that this time, if we went in, we might not be able to get out. I looked at Mellie and Scotty to see if they were okay. I started to say something but couldn't. I cleared my throat. Mellie and Scotty were looking at me as if hoping I would say, "Let's get out of here." I didn't, of course.

"C'mon, we can do this," I said.

"I hope you're right," said Scotty. Mellie nodded.

I grabbed each of their arms, and we proceeded up the steps. The steps made the same eerie creaking and cracking noises as before. They seemed louder this time, though.

The creaks and noises were getting on my nerves. "Ignore those. We're used to them," I said, trying to sound encouraging.

When we got to the front door, we stopped. No one wanted to open it. I looked at Mellie.

"I don't think so," she said.

I looked at Scotty.

"Are you kidding?" he asked.

I understood. I just nodded. I reached for the door. But before I touched it, the door slowly opened on its own.

"Are we used to that, too?" asked Scotty.

CHAPTER 24

We entered the house, fearful that something was going to happen. We stood quietly. We didn't hear anything but our own breathing.

"Well, here we are again," said Mellie.

"So far, so good," I said.

"Sure, it is," said Scotty.

"Right now, we have *something made of evil* and *tears without*," I said. "We need *tears within, the smoke of needles*, and *a possession of Victor's*. Let's look around and see if we can find anything that could fit those. We'll split up to make things go faster. Mellie, you start in the kitchen. Scotty, you begin in the back of the house, and I'll check the living room."

Mellie and Scotty nodded. Mellie and Scotty took two steps in the direction they were supposed to go. The next thing I knew, they were on either side of me.

"Okay, we'll go together," I said. "That's probably a better idea anyway."

We went room by room, stopping at the slightest noise. Afraid to go on.

We came across a man's pipe and some matches in the living room.

"What about these?" Mellie suggested. "The pipe could belong to Victor."

"The matches could be *the smoke of needles*," Scotty said. "When a match is lit, the fire could cause a sharp pain. Meaning something needle-sharp."

I thought about it. "I think the pipe and matches may be a bit of a stretch," I said. "I don't think Eleanor would keep a pipe of Victor's in her house. And even though fire from matches might cause a sharp pain, it just doesn't feel right. I don't think that's what she meant when she referred to *the smoke of needles*. We need to keep looking."

We entered the kitchen. At first glance, we couldn't see anything that seemed to go along with what Eleanor wrote.

"Maybe we have to dig a little deeper," I said. "Maybe the things we are looking for are not right in front of us. Let's check the cupboards and drawers. Kitchens are used for cooking, so smoke might fit."

"Right, and there are sharp or needle-pointed things in kitchens," said Mellie.

We felt we might be on to something. With renewed determination, we opened the cupboards and drawers. We found glasses and dishes, along with knives of various sizes. I was so focused on what we were doing that I didn't notice the smoke slowly rising from between the floorboards.

"Ouch," said Scotty, rubbing his fingers together. "This cupboard handle is hot."

"Yes," said Mellie, "These dishes are hot, too." She almost dropped one on the floor.

"It's getting warmer in here," I said as I unbuttoned the top button of my shirt.

"It sure is," said Scotty, sweat dripping down his face.

"What's going on?" Mellie asked, wiping the sweat off her forehead.

Suddenly, we heard laughter. Victor's evil laughter. Even though we were sweating, we froze in fear.

"Looking for needle-sharp things and smoke? Let me

help you find them," Victor roared with evil glee. And with that, knives from the drawers flew at Mellie, Scotty, and me. Missing us by inches! They flew by in a blur of motion. We felt the air move as they whipped by. They landed in the walls around us. There were so many of them, I couldn't believe they didn't hit us. There must have been a dozen knives sticking in the walls.

Black smoke from between the floorboards rose quickly and surrounded us, making it difficult to see and breathe. The floor was hot, almost too hot to stand on.

"We've got to get out of here! The house is on fire," I screamed.

"I can't see anything but smoke," cried Mellie.

"Which way?" Scotty yelled.

"I know the way. Grab on to me," I hollered. "Don't let go."

"Don't worry about that," Scotty shouted. He and Mellie grabbed onto me.

I couldn't see much of anything. My eyes were burning from the smoke and heat. But I remembered the way. Moving as quickly as I could, I finally reached the front door. "We made it," I screamed with relief.

I quickly grabbed the doorknob with my sleeve. It wouldn't open. I pulled and pulled. The door was locked!

CHAPTER 25

"It's locked," I screamed.

"What! That can't be," shrieked Mellie.

"We're cooked for sure!" hollered Scotty.

"We have one more chance," I yelled. "Hang on."

I got down low and crawled my way back through the house. I tried to open a window, but it was jammed. I needed to get to the back door. I could feel that Mellie and Scotty were getting weak from the heat and smoke. They were losing their grip on my arm. I knew that soon I wouldn't have the strength to get them out.

I fought my way through the heat and smoke, pulling my friends with me. Almost there.

"Ollie, I don't think I can make it," Mellie pleaded. I

felt her grip sliding down my arm.

"Hang on. We're almost to the back door!" I clenched my teeth and pulled Mellie and Scotty with all my determination. Just when I thought I wouldn't reach the door, something wet hit the top of my head.

I looked up. Water was dripping quickly down from the walls and ceilings. It was putting out the fire and smoke.

"*Tears from within,*" I whispered.

We made it to the back door.

"Thank you, Eleanor," I repeated over and over, as we fell out the back door and onto the ground. We were hacking and coughing, but we were out of the house.

When we were able to stand, I asked, "Are you guys okay?"

Mellie coughed but said, "Wet, but happy to be able to breathe again." She took in a couple of deep breaths.

"A bit well-done, but okay," Scotty said. "I thought we were going to end up looking like burnt toast."

"We almost did. Eleanor saved us with her tears," I said. "*Tears from within.*"

My hair was wet. Water dripped from my shirt. Mellie and Scotty were dripping water, also. "We now have a third piece of what Eleanor said we needed," I said.

After a few minutes, I turned back toward the house. I couldn't see any fire or smoke. Everything appeared quiet again. I went back into the house and found a jar in the kitchen cabinet. I grabbed it and went back outside. We squeezed as much of the water, Eleanor's tears, as we could into the jar. We put the jar in the backpack.

"Let's go back to the cabin and see if we can put this together somehow," I said.

CHAPTER 26

By the time we got back to our cabin, we were exhausted. Before we went inside, something near the bushes caught my attention. But I couldn't quite put my finger on it.

Scotty was so tired he could barely bring in the backpack. None of us could talk. We were too tired to even eat. We took off our wet clothes and went to bed early.

I didn't stir all night. I'm sure it was the same for Mellie and Scotty.

The next morning, we slept late, drained from the stress and adventure of the day before. When I got up, I went into the kitchen. Mellie and Scotty were already there. They looked tired but hopeful that we had one more thing that Eleanor wrote that we needed.

We had breakfast and then felt ready to discuss our situation. We pulled out Eleanor's diary, the amulet, and the handkerchief. We placed them on the table. Also, on the table were the bowl and the bark with the sap on it. In the bowl was the smashed creature. And we had the jar with Eleanor's tears.

"We have these," I said, pointing to everything on the table. "We're getting closer. Eleanor saved us yesterday with her tears that put out the fire and smoke, and now we have her *tears from within.*"

"We still need *the smoke of needles,*" said Mellie.

"And *a possession of Victor's,*" said Scotty. "We'll never end this curse without those."

As we were talking, Uncle John walked in. "Hey, sleepy heads, this country air must agree with you," he said with a smile. "You're getting plenty of rest. Enjoying yourselves?"

"Something like that," I said.

Mellie and Scotty smiled but didn't say anything.

Uncle John noticed the bowl on the table. "I didn't know you brought that bowl," he said. "I'm glad you're able to use it. It came from this area, you know."

I looked at Uncle John, unsure of what he was going

to say. Mellie and Scotty listened intently.

"What do you mean?" I asked. "I thought you got this on one of your research expeditions."

"Yes, I did," said Uncle John. "The one I did here years ago. I told you before that I had been here. I was exploring one of the caves I told you to check out. That's when I found it."

"You found it in one of the caves? Was it dropped there by a tourist?" I asked, though I feared I knew the answer. Understanding started to dawn on me.

"Oh, no," said Uncle John. "You remember the story I told you about Eleanor, Robert, and Victor?"

One by one, we slowly nodded.

"I showed the bowl to experts at the historical center in town. They said the bowl was very old and probably belonged to Victor. They said that the faded lion and shield on the bowl are his family crest. They speculated that it could be the bowl Victor used when he practiced black magic." Uncle John laughed. "They looked serious, but I thought they were kidding around. They knew I was a tourist, and I assumed they were just telling me the local story. I mean, who would believe a story like that was true?" He laughed again and shook his head.

"Who would?" I chuckled nervously.

Soon Uncle John left to continue his research.
I knew more was to come.

CHAPTER 27

At first, no one spoke. The reality of what Uncle John had said slowly sank in.

We looked at the bowl on the table. Then we backed away from it. Scotty went to get a stick from outside and poked the bowl. Nothing happened.

"Wait a minute," I said. "What are we thinking? We've been touching this bowl all the time. I used it at home a lot. This bowl isn't going to hurt us. In fact, if it is Victor's bowl, it will help us."

"You're right, Ollie," said Mellie. "We have another piece we need to break the curse."

"The other thing we still need to figure out is *the smoke of needles*," Scotty said. "Nothing we've thought of so far fits that."

"When we got back here yesterday, I felt like I had the answer just before me," I said. "But I was so tired that whatever it was quickly disappeared. We're close. I can feel it. If only I could remember what I was thinking."

"Did it have anything to do with the fire?" Mellie asked.

I thought about it. "No, I don't think it was about the fire or smoke," I said.

"What about the needles?" Scotty asked. "Were you thinking about them?"

I frowned, aggravated that the thought eluded me. "Not needles, exactly, but sharp points. Something about sharp, pointed needles," I said.

Just as the memory was about to come to me, Scotty asked, "What is that noise?"

"What noise?" asked Mellie.

"I don't hear anything," I said.

"Listen," Scotty commanded. Then, from somewhere inside the cabin, we heard a whirling or spinning sound. "*That* noise," Scotty whispered.

Then, as if whatever made that sound heard him, the noise became louder.

"What is that?" asked Mellie, concern in her voice.

We went to investigate. Walking down the hallway to our rooms, we saw something covering the bedroom doors. We slowly approached the first door. Afraid of what it was.

I was the first to realize what it was. "It's the sticky coarse rope from the maggot creatures from the cave! The ones that didn't have a head! Run!" I yelled.

Suddenly, as if from a nightmare, hundreds of maggot creatures were everywhere. It looked like they were coming up through the floorboards and out of the cracks in the walls. Leaving the sticky coarse rope everywhere, they scurried quickly from one room to the next.

Mellie, Scotty, and I ran to the front door. It was totally enclosed by the rope.

"They're cocooning us in!" Mellie screamed.

Not knowing where to go or what to do, we backed up. We were totally surrounded by the sticky rope.

"How did they get in here?" Scotty bellowed.

"I thought your Uncle John said the cave entrance would be sealed," Mellie yelled.

"This one wasn't!" Scotty shouted in a high-pitched tone.

"Remember, Victor practiced black magic. He must have figured out a way," I hollered.

Scotty yelled in panic, "Evil Destroyer, think of something! Get us out of this!"

My thoughts were going a mile a minute, trying frantically to devise a solution. Then our backs hit the kitchen table. We had nowhere to go!

CHAPTER 28

"Scotty, get the handkerchief!" I yelled.

At first, Scotty, frozen in terror, didn't understand what I was talking about. Then hope broke through his fear. He turned and picked up the handkerchief from the table.

"Throw it at the creatures!" I screamed.

Scotty threw the handkerchief into the mass of the maggot creatures. When he did, there was loud screeching and shrieking. The creatures scurried back into the floorboards and cracks in the walls, climbing over each other to get out as quickly as possible. Within a minute or so, all the creatures disappeared. The handkerchief worked. But we were still cocooned—alive.

I retrieved the handkerchief from the floor and gave it back to Scotty. "Take everything on the table," I said. "We're going to need it all. When I give the signal, Scotty, you stay in front of us and use the handkerchief to make a path out of here."

"I don't want to be . . ." Scotty started, but then he remembered the handkerchief only worked for him.

I grabbed the diary and the jar that contained Eleanor's tears. Mellie took the amulet, the bowl with the smashed creature, and the bark. We put them all in the backpack. Scotty had the handkerchief. We hesitated for a second. The sticky rope was everywhere.

I nodded and said, "Get ready. Let's get out of here."

Scotty moved faster than Mellie or I had ever seen him move. As he touched the sticky rope with the handkerchief, the rope dissolved. The rope dissolved off the handkerchief too. Soon we were out of the house and running for our bikes.

As we reached our bikes, I turned and looked back. That's when it dawned on me. I remembered what had been bothering me so much earlier. I ran back toward the house.

Mellie screamed, "Ollie, what are you doing? Are you crazy?"

"Those creatures might come back!" yelled Scotty.

I didn't stop. I knew what I had to do.

I ran to the area that was overgrown with bushes. The bushes with berries, prickers, and thorns. Pointed, sharp thorns! That's what Eleanor meant by needles. The last thing we needed had been around us all along!

CHAPTER 29

Mellie and Scotty caught up with me. They grabbed me by the arms and tried to pull me away.

"No," I shouted. "Just start cutting. These are the needles. *The needles!*"

At first, Mellie and Scotty looked at me like I was crazy. Then they understood. They helped me cut some of the thorns off the bushes. Our hands were getting cut, but we didn't care.

"How do you know this is right?" asked Mellie.

"Uncle John told us people used to burn certain plants and bushes . . . the thornier and pricklier, the better. The smoke was supposed to ward off evil."

"Victor," Scotty sighed.

"Eleanor stated *the smoke of needles* was needed to help break the curse," I said.

"Right," Mellie affirmed.

When we had enough to fill the bottom of the bowl, I said, "Let's finish this."

We got on our bikes. But all of a sudden, the ground started to shift. The trees began to shake.

"Oh no!" yelled Scotty.

"Go. Go. Go!" I hollered.

We rode fast, faster than we thought possible. A black, whirling wind was chasing us. I could feel the air rushing up behind us. We felt a strong tremor. The ground behind us broke apart. Large cracks in the earth were racing toward us. The sky lit up with an eerie glow. Lightning and thunder were all around us. All the while, we could hear Victor's wicked laugh.

I could feel an evil energy going through my body. It was frightening. I hoped and prayed we were going to make it. Finally, we saw Eleanor's house.

"We're not going to make it," Mellie screamed. "We're going to get swallowed up!"

"We're almost there," I hollered.

At last, we got to Eleanor's house. I grabbed the backpack and ran to the front door. I turned the door handle.

The door opened easily. We rushed inside. Barely able to believe we had made it.

We ran into the living room and placed everything on the table. I set the bowl in the middle of the table. The smashed creature was still in it. I poured some of Eleanor's tears into the bowl. As I was doing this, the front door slammed open. We all jumped.

"We have company," Scotty warned. "And it's not the kind we want."

"Hurry, Ollie," Mellie pleaded.

I quickly scraped off some of the tears of sap from the piece of bark Scotty cut off the limb. I put it in the bowl.

A strong wind whipped through the living room. Pictures flew off the walls. Furniture tipped over. Items on shelves sailed across the room.

When I sprinkled the thorns into the mix, we heard a scream of rage.

Victor suddenly appeared before us. His face was etched with rage. "No!" he shrieked. He lifted his arms and sent a yellow streak of lightning at me.

I screamed and jumped out of the way. I felt an intense heat as the bolt flew inches above me. The top of my head felt hot. I gingerly touched it. It hurt. My hair was singed. The bowl almost went flying. But Mellie and

Scotty grabbed it as it lifted off the table.

I quickly mixed all the ingredients in the bowl: *something made of evil, tears within and tears without, needles for smoke,* all in a bowl that was *a possession of Victor's.*

Then I pulled out my lighter. I ignited the contents. Billows and billows of smoke rose into the air. I swiftly opened Eleanor's diary to the page where she dictated the chant that must be said.

"Quick, hold hands," I yelled. We surrounded the bowl. Mellie, Scotty, and I read aloud from the diary:

"Eleanor and Robert's love was true
It is now time for them to start anew
Break this curse that holds them tight
Let our love be strong to release them
So their love can again shine bright."

"I will destroy all of you!" Victor screeched, "No! No! No!"

At first, nothing happened. All was quiet. Victor put his head back and started to laugh wildly. Then he stopped. He stood staring at us with pure black hatred dripping from his eyes.

He smiled an evil smile. "Now you are mine," he

cursed. "You will feel great pain for helping Eleanor. You can join her after I am done with you! There won't be much left of you to help her again."

Mellie, Scotty, and I could only stare at Victor in horror. Our arms dropped to our sides. Our chant didn't work. We failed Eleanor and Robert. And now, after Victor was done with us, we were going to suffer the same fate as them! My brain couldn't even imagine what he meant by that.

I couldn't figure out what had gone wrong. We had mixed everything together like we were supposed to. We said the chant Eleanor had written down. Maybe what we mixed together wasn't the right stuff. I didn't know.

As Victor took a step toward us, I had an idea. "Mellie, grab the amulet. Get in between Scotty and me."

Mellie grabbed the amulet and did what I asked.

"Scotty, grab my hands."

He did.

"Mellie, push on the jewel."

Mellie put her finger on the jewel and pushed down on it. As she did, I pleaded, "Help, help, please help!"

For one moment, all was silent. Then there was movement all around us. The walls started to spin. Faster and faster.

"I think I'm going to be sick," said Scotty.

"Don't let go," I yelled. "Close your eyes."

We all closed our eyes. I could feel my hair being blown wildly around my head.

"Ollie!" Mellie shouted, as she grabbed on to me.

Scotty screamed, "What is happening?"

"Just keep your eyes closed and hang on to each other," I yelled.

The spinning of the room seemed to last forever. Then just as it had started, it stopped. I was afraid to open my eyes. Fearful of what I might see or not see.

CHAPTER 30

I peeked with one eye. What I saw made my heart sing. "It's okay, Mellie and Scotty." I beamed. "You can open your eyes now."

Before us stood Eleanor and Robert. Smiling at us. Eleanor was even more beautiful than in the picture. Her hair was a gorgeous shade of brown that perfectly matched her stunning brown eyes. Robert was very handsome. His clothes were rather plain, but he had natural good looks. He was tall and fit. He had black wavy hair and striking blue eyes. They were a beautiful couple.

Eleanor looked at us and smiled broadly. "Thank you," she said, almost in a whisper. Eleanor then gently

touched Mellie's hand and took the amulet from Mellie. I wasn't sure what was going to happen next.

Eleanor then turned to face Victor. Her face turned from joyous to a very stern look.

Victor stared at us in stunned disbelief. Not saying anything.

Eleanor took Robert's hand. "Victor, you tried to destroy our love with your jealousy and hate," she said. "But our love is timeless. You separated us and bound us to our prisons forever. Close but far apart. Now it is time for you to pay for what you did to us."

And with that, Eleanor raised the amulet toward Victor. "May the price you pay be the curse you put upon us," she declared. "Victor, may you be bound here for all time. Never to know happiness. All your riches, everything you cherish, will be right outside, so you can watch the elements destroy them slowly, over time, unable to do anything about it. You are powerless."

Victor looked like he couldn't believe that his hold on them was now broken. "You will never escape me," he cried out.

Eleanor smiled and pressed the jewel on the amulet. "You will regret this!" Victor screamed.

White smoke swirled into the air and surrounded

him. We watched as he struggled to escape it, thrashing his arms and kicking his legs, but the swirling smoke held him tightly. Around and around him it went until it totally covered him. The white smoke made very little noise but appeared to be very forceful. We could hear him screaming and cursing until . . . all was silent.

Eleanor smiled and pointed to the picture of her on the wall. Now, it was replaced by a picture of Victor. He was snarling. Forever.

Eleanor and Robert looked at each other; their affection and happiness shone brightly in their eyes. Their love for each other was so strong and so pure that I could feel it. It brought tears to our eyes. After a few moments, Eleanor and Robert turned to us.

Mellie, Scotty, and I had been holding onto each other.

"We will always be in your debt," Robert said. "Without you, the curse would never have been broken."

"Your goodness and love for each other saved us," said Eleanor. "Always keep that love in your heart. It may save you one day, as you saved us."

"What will happen to you now?" I asked.

"We will love each other and be together. Forever. Always," said Robert.

"Just like we planned and dreamed of doing," Eleanor added.

"Thank you all for what you did for us," said Robert.

"Yes, thank you for your courage and for saving us," said Eleanor.

Mellie, Scotty, and I could only smile. Tears swam in our eyes.

"You won't be needing these any longer," Eleanor said, pointing to the amulet, diary, and handkerchief. She smiled at us again, "We will be forever grateful."

And with that, white smoke covered the amulet, diary, and handkerchief. It then whirled and swirled and surrounded Robert and Eleanor. One minute they were there. The next minute they were gone.

For the next several moments, Mellie, Scotty, and I just stood there, stunned. Nobody said anything. I was very happy for Eleanor and Robert, but it seemed like we had lost a friend. But they will be eternally happy together.

Finally, Mellie spoke. "Wow," was all she could say.

"Yeah," said Scotty.

"Unbelievable," I said.

Mellie, Scotty, and I walked out of the house toward our bikes. There was no creaking on the steps as we walked down them. When we got to the bottom of the steps, I thought I heard something.

"Stop. Listen," I said.

With all of us stopped, we could hear a low whimper. Then the whimper turned into a combination of howling, cursing, and crying. But this time, it was a man crying— Victor.

"It looks like it is still the Weeping House," said Scotty.

"That's the happiest sound I've ever heard," Mellie said.

We all laughed, got on our bikes, and rode back to the cabin.

CHAPTER 31

The next day, we sat in the kitchen, talking about all that had happened.

"Each of us was needed for the diary, amulet, and handkerchief to work," I said. "We needed to work together to break the curse."

"It wasn't easy, but we were able to figure out all the things Eleanor wrote about," said Mellie. "Those things, along with our goodness and love, were needed to defeat Victor and free Eleanor and Robert."

"We almost didn't," said Scotty. "If you hadn't figured out about the thorns as needles, Ollie, things would have ended differently."

"The answer was in front of us all the time," I said. "It

was by mere chance that the idea of needles and thorns made sense. We had already mentioned needles being sharp. There was something in the back of my mind that I couldn't quite remember. Then all I could see were the thorns. It must have been the adrenaline from the fear of being cocooned that caused everything to click into place."

"But what about those creatures?" Scotty asked. "Should we tell someone about them?"

I thought about it. "I don't think that's necessary," I said. "I'm pretty sure it was like we reasoned before. Victor, with his black magic, could conjure up whatever he wanted. He created those creatures to get rid of us. Once he's gone, so are the creatures."

"But couldn't he conjure up something while he's stuck in the house?" asked Scotty.

"I don't think so," I said. "Eleanor used the amulet to lock him in that picture and the house. It must be powerful enough to keep him there."

"Unless someone somehow releases him," said Mellie.

"Let's hope not," Scotty replied.

At that moment, Uncle John walked in. "What are you guys talking about?" he asked.

"Just about what we've been doing while we were here," I said.

"I'm sorry I've been so busy during our trip," said Uncle John. "I did find all the information I needed. I hope you've been doing interesting things and having fun."

"You wouldn't believe it if we told you," I said.

"Are you guys ready to go home?" he asked.

I looked at Mellie and Scotty. They nodded.

"We've had enough excitement here," I said.

It took only a few minutes to pack up the car. I couldn't find my bowl. I think I might have left it at Eleanor's house, but I didn't remember seeing it when we left there. *Oh well . . .* I thought. *It did its job.*

We checked the cabin one last time to make sure we didn't leave anything behind. As we stood together in the kitchen, I held my fist out to Mellie and Scotty. They held their fists out as well, and we fist bumped. "Friends Forever," we said together. We left with our arms around each other.

"On to the next adventure?" I asked.

"Sounds good," said Mellie.

"No," said Scotty, but he smiled.

EPILOGUE

Months later, I was lying on the grass in my backyard. It was getting dark, but I didn't want to go in
just yet. It was such a nice, warm, peaceful night. I was
looking at the stars. I noticed some of them seemed to
be twinkling oddly.

Are they saying hello or trying to get my attention? I
wondered. *Could they be trying to warn me about something?* Then I thought, *Don't be ridiculous. You're in your
own backyard.*

I continued to stare at the stars. My thoughts were a
million miles away.

Suddenly, the temperature dropped, and the wind
picked up. An unnerving chill spread through the air. I

felt uneasy. Then I thought I heard something. I couldn't quite make it out. I sat up. My heart started to beat a little faster. I wasn't sure why.

The sound became a little louder. It sounded like whirling and spinning, and it seemed to be getting closer. Then out of nowhere, something flew through the air and hit my foot. It was a bowl. *My bowl?* I thought. *No way.* That bowl had been missing since we broke the curse.

I lifted the bowl with shaking fingers. I was breathing fast.

It can't be, I thought. I turned the bowl in my hands. That's when I saw it.

Even though it was nearly dark, I could just make out a faded lion and shield.

It is . . .

ACKNOWLEDGMENTS

I would like to thank the following people for their invaluable help in the creation, editing, and publishing of this book. Your assistance is sincerely appreciated.

- Marlo Garnsworthy
- Darren Wheeling
- Ben Simpson
- Gillian Barth
- Shannon Sullivan

ABOUT THE AUTHOR

F. P. LaRue is the author of the Scary Shivers mystery series. These adventure mysteries are written for middle-grade children and are designed to show them that reading is fun! She loves scary stories and particularly enjoys sharing her own frightening tales. F. P. is a member of the Society of Children's Book Writers and Illustrators.

Before writing children's books, F. P.'s career was in education. She progressed from being a teacher to the dean of academic affairs for a small Michigan college. When not writing, F. P. loves to travel, having visited all fifty states and fifty-four countries worldwide.

F. P. hopes her stories inspire children to discover

the wondrous adventures reading can bring—no matter their age.

You can find out more about F. P. LaRue and the next Scary Shivers Mystery below.

www.FPLaRue.com

www.ScaryShivers.com

 FPLaRue